# Piercehaven

## ROBIN MERRILL

New Creation Publishing

New Creation Publishing
Madison, Maine

This novel is a work of fiction. Names, characters, businesses, organizations, places, events, and incidents are either the products of the author's imagination or used in a fictitious manner. Any resemblance to actual persons, living or dead, or actual events is purely coincidental.

# Chapter 1

She had expected it to be a poetic voyage. She had expected sunshine and whitecaps, a sea song to serenade her as she sailed toward her new home.

But from where she sat, she could barely see over the bow.

If she could have, she would have seen that the ferry was enshrouded by a thick fog.

They had packed their cargo of cars and people so efficiently, so compactly, she thought she would have to make a scene just to get out of her own car. She sat there thinking, trying to figure out how she would squeeze out between her driver's side door and the giant steel beam it would be pressed up against once she opened it. Scooting over to the passenger side wouldn't help, as that door was pushed up against the gunwale.

# PIERCEHAVEN

She felt trapped. In so many different ways.

She had been warned about teaching in a small school. In rural Maine. She had been told that people would be watching her every move. That there was nowhere to hide on an island. But it wasn't those attentive eyes she wanted to avoid at the moment, though the ferry could quite well be full of them.

She was most worried about catching the eye of the man in the pickup truck parked only inches away from her, whose Ford was pressed up against the other side of the steel beam. If she made like toothpaste and tried to squirt out of her Toyota, surely he would see her, and surely she would die of embarrassment. Not because he was handsome, though he certainly appeared to be from where she sat, but because he had a Bible on his dashboard. And this impressed her.

She'd never known anyone to drive around with a Bible on his dashboard. And though the man was currently staring down at his smart phone, probably playing Candy Crush, it still had to be a good sign that he had a Bible so readily within reach.

So she stared straight ahead, wondering if she was really going to spend the ninety-minute ride trapped in her car, though, apparently all the cool kids, e.g., Bible-dashboard-guy, were doing it.

She was too nervous to sleep, her phone battery was too low to play Candy Crush (she would charge it in the car, but her cigarette lighter hole had long ago given up the ghost), and she didn't have a Bible handy.

She knew the voyage offered breathtaking views of coastal Maine. She'd seen them before, when she'd made the trip for her job interview, which had been so far beyond strange that she almost hadn't taken the job.

The part-time superintendent and the very, very old principal had sat her down in a very, very old room with cement walls, no air conditioning, and a lazy ceiling fan. The one window had been open, but it didn't help. The room had smelled like dirty socks. Yet she had tried to face her interviewers bravely, as they asked her a series of increasingly bizarre questions.

She'd been to so many other teaching job interviews, she was used to the normal questions, the logical ones, the expected ones: what is your greatest strength; describe your greatest challenge; what is your behavior management philosophy; how will you engage the unengaged student. But these questions weren't those. These were: how many people went to your high school (about 1200, still fairly small by national standards); what sports did you play in high school (zip, zadda, zilch, as they'd used to say in her hometown); what do you do to relax (she'd said read; they'd looked suspicious); and finally, where would you live.

"We could set you up with a place," the superintendent had said.

She'd been nonplussed. Did this mean she had the job?

"What I mean is, if this works out, we could provide you with an option. It's a small house, owned by members of the school board, but they would rent it to you. We just bring it up now because it's difficult for new teachers to find housing. There aren't many apartments on the island. And there are a few houses for sale, but those are usually out of a new teacher's reach."She remembered nodding, wondering if he'd really said the house was owned by school board *members*, plural? As in, they co-owned a house? Wasn't that a bit strange?

But, back then, she'd been nervous, sweating through her pantsuit, and wanting to get out of there, so she'd just smiled agreeably. Then they had exchanged clammy handshakes and sent her on her way. She'd been fairly certain that she would never hear from them again, and tried to enjoy the ferry ride home.

But the principal had called her the next morning and offered her a job. And without hesitation, she had verbally accepted.

She'd been looking for a full-time teaching gig for six years. She'd been an ed tech, a tutor, an adult ed teacher, and a substitute, and all of those gigs had really, truly stunk. So she didn't care how bad it was teaching in a tiny school on an island—she would have her own classroom, her own students. And she couldn't wait.

So why, now, staring out into the fog, did she have this sense of foreboding in her gut? *Just nerves*, she thought, trying to shake them off. She saw Bible-dashboard-guy cross in front of her windshield and then expertly scale the ladderway, three steps at a time, up to the next deck. She looked to her left to make sure that had really been him, and sure enough, his truck sat empty. *Now or never*, she thought, and creaked her door open. Then she tried to slide out through the small opening, frantically looking around for anyone who might be observing. There was no one. She sucked in her belly and pushed, and then, she was free. Standing outside her car. In the damp, salty

7

morning air. She shut her door and only then realized she might not be so lucky as to be able to slide back in unobserved.

*Oh well, too late now.* She followed Bible-dashboard-guy up the starboard ladderway, though not nearly as nimbly as he had ascended, and found herself alone on the upper deck. And not only could she not see Bible-dashboard-guy, she couldn't see *anything.* The boat could have been alone in the middle of the ocean for all she knew. She couldn't see the island up ahead, though it might not have been visible yet anyway, it was so far from the mainland. She turned around and couldn't see the mainland. She looked over the side. She could see the water. *Well there. At least there's that.*

# Chapter 2

They had given her an address for the house, telling her to just "move right in," that they would take care of the details later. She was terrified that she didn't yet know what the rent was, but the housing arrangement hadn't sounded optional, so she'd just gone with it.

She had saved what little cell battery she had so that she could use the GPS to find the place. But when she turned her phone on, she realized she had no signal. *How is that even possible? So the whole island is cellphoneless? Might make classroom management easier.*

She hated to stop, but she didn't see any other options. She had already driven away from the ferry station by the time she realized her predicament, which was too bad, as that was the logical place to ask for directions. Instead, she stopped in front of Marget's Grocery.

# PIERCEHAVEN

*This is the smallest grocery store I've ever seen*, she realized, stepping inside. A small bell sounded over her head. *How quaint*. The woman running the only register looked up at her and smiled. The man checking out stared at her and didn't smile. She thought maybe she ought to buy something. She'd arrived to her new home with very little food. She grabbed a cart and started to explore. But the bananas were ninety-nine cents per pound. The milk, seven dollars per gallon. She had been excited when they had quoted her the salary offer—the lowest salary allowed by law, which was still almost twice what she had been making with all her pretend-teaching gigs. But now she panicked at the thought of how much it would cost her to eat. And so, when she approached the checkout, her cart only held one half-gallon of milk, three bananas, and a large box of Ramen.

"Good morning," the cashier said. Her nametag said Marget. "I don't think I've seen you before?"

"I'm Emily." She smiled, honestly pleased with the friendly reception.

"Hi, Emily!" Marget said. "You wouldn't be the new English teacher would you?"

Emily's jaw dropped.

Marget chuckled. "Don't be alarmed. I knew we were getting a new English teacher, and someone had said you were young. We don't get many new people around here, so I just put two and two together. That'll be $12.85."

Still feeling a smidge stunned, Emily rummaged in her purse for the money. She handed her a twenty.

Marget counted back her change and then said, "Welcome to the island."

This reminded Emily of why she had stopped at the store in the first place. "Could you give me directions? I'm looking for Songbird Lane."

"Oh, of course. You just want to follow this road," she said, pointing to the direction Emily had been going, away from the ferry terminal, "for about four miles. There will be a boatyard, and I think Songbird is the second turn after that, maybe the third, on your right. But don't worry, you can't get lost. There's really only one road, and it just loops around the island."

"Thank you," Emily said, taking her bags. "I'm sure I'll find it." But she wasn't sure at all. She was a bundle of nerves, and hated herself for it.

Even though she slowed to a crawl at Murray's Boatyard, she still drove by Songbird

Lane. She put the car in reverse and backed up the empty road. Then she turned right.

Songbird Lane was a narrow dirt drive with grass growing in the middle. She was looking for 5 Songbird Lane, so she figured it would be coming up soon, but as she rolled along the dirt path, she realized she was wrong. It felt like miles before she went by the first sign of civilization—a trailer on her right. A pickup and a four-wheeler sat in the driveway. Two tricycles and what looked like seventy thousand lobster traps decorated the lawn.

A quarter of a mile beyond that she drove by a funny-shaped, dilapidated house on her left. It looked like something designed by stoners and also appeared to be abandoned, but then as she drove by, she noticed a dog tied to the porch. She drove a half mile, only scraping the bottom of her car on one boulder, and then a cute, tiny A-frame came into sight. She didn't think this was hers, but as she got closer, she saw a wooden "5" nailed next to the door.

*This is it.* The driveway was barely long enough to pull her Corolla into. She turned off the engine and looked around. No neighbors in sight. The road narrowed to almost nothing past her driveway. This was truly the end of the line. She got out of the car and approached the house with some wariness, suddenly overcome with the desire to adopt a dog. A big dog. She wondered if the island had an animal shelter.

They'd told her they would leave it unlocked, the key on the kitchen table. The door knob turned easily, but the door stuck. Probably just the moisture in the air. She lowered her shoulder and pushed, and it gave way.

Once she stepped inside, she felt better, because the house was *cute*. Straight ahead was a cozy living room, complete with woodstove, couch, and cushioned armchair. No TV, which was fine by her. To her right, the kitchen, complete with range, fridge, a counter that ran between the two, and a table with four chairs. She had no idea who would sit there, but just in case, she had the room. A door stood open at the far side of the living room. She walked through it, into the world's smallest bathroom.

A spiral staircase led to the loft, which held a full-sized bed and a dresser. She loved it. She loved it so much that her rent panic skyrocketed. No need to get attached if this wasn't meant to be. She found the keys on the kitchen table as promised, atop a single piece of paper that read:

Welcome to the island, Emily! If this space will work for you, you are welcome to stay here for as long as you are serving in our school. We just ask you to keep it in good shape! Best, Lauren P.S. If you need anything, call me at 555-4314.

*No way.* Did this mean rent-free? She put the paper down and looked around. It was too good to be true. She *loved* this place! *Now I can afford to buy groceries!*

She felt like dancing. Instead, she opened the windows and began carrying her few bags inside. They had told her fully-furnished, so she didn't have much stuff, and it didn't take her long. Then she stood in the middle of her new living room, wondering just how she could call Lauren, or anyone for that matter, with no cell service. She wandered back into the kitchen and noticed an actual landline phone on the wall next to the fridge. She hadn't seen one of those in years. She picked it up. Sure enough, a dial tone. She looked at it. A number was written on it: 555-5774. Apparently, she had a new phone number.

New number. New home. New job. New everything. All she needed was the dog.

# Chapter 3

The school, which housed grades K through 12, looked like two long mobile homes stuck together to form a T.

She'd been here once before, of course, for her interview, but now it looked different somehow. Back then, she'd been a bit haughty pulling up the long driveway. She'd laughed at the small school, thinking it backward and maybe even piteous.

But now it was her home. Or it would be, starting in about five minutes. And that felt mightily strange. She looked at the small building in the early morning sunlight and thought, *This? This is it? This is where I'm going to build my life now? How can this be? What will this be?*

She parked the car in the corner of the one parking lot and, with an unsteady stomach, headed into the building.

No one met her at the door, and she paused to recognize how absurd that expectation had been. This wasn't church. She looked around the empty foyer, wondering where to go. The foyer was still dark, except for the trophy cases that lined each of the walls. These were backlit, and were full of team photos, basketball hoop nets, and gold balls.

She saw some glass windows that were probably a main office and she headed that way.

A woman sat behind a giant desk covered with neat piles of papers and binders.

"Good morning," Emily said.

The woman looked up. "Oh, good morning. Are you Miss Morse?"

Emily nodded. "I am." She took what she hoped looked like confident strides over to the desk and stuck out her hand.

The woman took it. "I'm Julie." Julie handed Emily a folder. "Here's our new teacher welcome package. If you have any questions, please let me know. The first staff meeting"— she glanced at the clock—"starts in about ten minutes. Do you know where your classroom is?"

Emily shook her head. "I haven't been there yet."

"Larry!" Julie hollered out into the hallway, startling Emily more than a little. "This is the new English teacher. Can you show her her classroom?"

Larry nodded and walked away.

*Am I supposed to follow him?* Emily looked at Julie for direction. She offered none. "OK, thanks," Emily said, and then followed Larry down the hallway. Judging from his outfit and the slew of keys hanging off one belt loop, Emily assumed Larry was a custodian. She sped up, but she still didn't catch him before he stopped in front of a closed door. He opened it and then walked away. Emily watched him go. Apparently, this was her room? She looked inside. It certainly looked like a language arts classroom, based on the scores of paperbacks lining the walls. She stepped inside and smiled. This was it. Finally. Her own space. She shut the door. Then wondered why she'd done so. She had only minutes, and she had no idea where the meeting was. She crossed the room to her desk and looked around. She drew a sharp breath. She actually had an ocean view out her classroom window, and it was gorgeous. She hadn't expected it because they weren't very close to the shore here, but the school sat on a hill that afforded some spectacular scenery. She envisioned herself staring out the window during her prep period, when she was supposed to be grading papers.

Emily couldn't remember ever wanting to be anything other than a teacher. She had grown up in the church, known about the great commission for as long as she could remember, and when her friends dreamed of growing up to be missionaries in Africa, Emily had always thought, *Wouldn't it be easier to just be a teacher?*

She took one last look out the window and then headed out to locate the faculty meeting.

It was in the gym. She followed the few people she saw into the large open space, which turned out to be the smallest gym she'd ever seen. It was a gym—it had basketball hoops at least—but it also had tiled floors instead of hardwood. And in the middle of the room sat two fold-out bench-style cafeteria tables. Each was filling up and she made her way to the end of one and slid into a vacant spot. This wasn't exactly what she'd expected a faculty meeting to look like.

The man sitting across from her said, "You must be the new language arts teacher?"

Only when she looked up at him did she see that he was kind of cute. She smiled. "I am. Emily," she said, and stuck out her hand.

He took it, and held it just a beat longer than normal.

"I'm Kyle. Social studies."

"Nice to meet you, Kyle."

"You nervous?"

"More like terrified."

Kyle laughed, revealing perfectly straight teeth that somehow made his goatee look more dapper.

She briefly wondered if dapperer was a word.

"Where are you from?" Kyle asked.

"Plainfield."

"Ah," he said.

"You've heard of it?"

"Well, yeah. Only because of the university. Is that where you went?"

"It is," Emily said, her embarrassment obvious.

"Oh, don't knock the state schools," Kyle said, still smiling. "I quickly learned that a state education will equip you for this job perfectly adequately, and you aren't saddled with the student loans of the private schools."

"Where did you go?"

"Colby."

"Oh, wow."

"Yes, that's what I say every month when I open my student loan bill. But really, it is overkill. You'll be just fine with what you've got. In fact, you were probably ready to teach these guys immediately after graduating from high school."

Emily was surprised, and didn't know what to say.

"Sorry." Kyle chuckled. "Was that unprofessional? Maybe I haven't been teaching long enough to be so cynical. Oh wait, yes I have. You see"—he leaned across the table toward her—"what I mean to say is, none of them actually *want* to learn, so it doesn't matter what you offer them, they won't take it."

She was still surprised, but tried to hide it. "I see," she said.

He smirked. "No, you don't, and that's OK. You will see it soon enough. Just do the best you can, don't have great expectations, and you'll be golden. Best case scenario, you convince one kid once in a while to get the bleep off the island. Worst case scenario, your check still cashes."

Emily saw the principal walking toward the podium and panicked a little. She thought she was learning far more from Kyle than she would from him. "They don't want to leave the island?"

Kyle's laugh sounded bitter. "Oh, they sure don't. They want to win state championships, graduate, and make basketball babies."

Principal Hogan cleared his throat at the podium. "Welcome, everyone, to a brand-new school year."

As the faculty offered some paltry applause, Kyle leaned toward her and said, "I mean babies who play basketball, not babies who *are* basketballs. That would just be weird." Then Kyle winked at her, leaned back, and turned his attention to the front of the room.

Piercehaven was known around the state for one reason: basketball. Especially girls' basketball.

Other islands closer to the mainland were famous for lighthouses, seafood restaurants, and bed and breakfasts that served lobster omelets, but the word "Piercehaven" was almost always associated with Maine's favorite winter sport.

For reasons she had never had cause to wonder about, the small island school held more state championships than any other school in the state. For the last twenty years, the Piercehaven Panthers had won more state championships than they had lost. And

21

apparently, she had just learned, they did it all from a weird tiled floor.

She forced her eyes front, and forced her ears to listen to Mr. Hogan. As he spoke, Julie wandered around passing out schedules. They had two workshop days, Monday and Tuesday, and then Wednesday the doors would open to the kids. Emily's stomach flipped at the thought, but that thought was quickly followed by another: *It'll be OK. You've got a friend now, a friend who isn't going to judge you with high expectations. He'll help.*

She looked at the schedule. Her morning would be spent learning about behavior management and then bullying prevention. Then the afternoon was dedicated to teachers getting their classrooms ready. Tomorrow morning: assessment planning, curriculum development, and then more time in the classroom. Though of course she wanted to get her classroom ready, she hoped she could invest at least a little of that time fraternizing with the social studies teacher.

Emily had to look past Kyle to see Mr. Hogan, so this gave her the perfect opportunity to check him out discreetly. He *was* cute, though she wished he wasn't so skinny. Not that she was fat. She wasn't. She was just kind of ... *thick*. She always had been. Her mother claimed she had been born that way. Her grandmother told her she had good "birthing hips." Despite this helpful commentary, Emily had always felt as though her body was just a little too ... *there*. Even without much actual fat on her, she still wore size ten pants, and they were always still too tight across the bottom. Today she wore an A-line skirt.

The day after she'd been offered the job, she'd spent some money—OK, that wasn't quite true—she'd spent some *credit* to update her wardrobe. She'd wanted to look professional. Confident. Like a real teacher.

Now, looking around the room, she wondered why she'd bothered. She counted nineteen people, and most of them were wearing jeans. A few were even in windpants. She realized she was overdressed. *Oh well, better over than under*. She wondered why there were so many people for such a small school, but after a few seconds of pondering this, she figured this must be *all* the teachers for *all* the grades, K through 12. She figured she was looking at every teacher on the island. Then she wondered why there were so *few* teachers.

The greetings and announcements over, Mr. Hogan dismissed them for a break. Kyle took her by the elbow and said conspiratorially, "Do you want me to introduce you to people, or just point at them and talk about them?"

She giggled. "You can just point and talk."

He pointed at an older woman who was knitting something big enough to be a parachute. "That's our Ed Tech III. That's right. We only have one. She'll be in your classroom at some point, but she's wonderful. Been here forever. Knows everyone. Is very supportive of teachers. But that"—he pointed to another woman—"is our Ed Tech II. She's also nice, but will tell Mr. Hogan everything that happens in your classroom. She's sort of a spy." He continued pointing and explaining. The math teacher was also new. So was the science teacher. So was the second grade teacher. The fourth grade teacher looked to be at least a hundred years old.

She noticed a balding man in wind pants staring at them. "Who's that?"

"Ugh. *That* is our phys ed teacher, our athletic director, and our girls' basketball coach. He's kind of a big deal, but not nearly as big of a deal as he thinks he is. Milton Darling. He's a few years older than me. Was a thousand point scorer. Most of the island thinks he walks on water."

"Do the girls like him?"

Kyle looked at her. "What do you mean?"

She thought it had been a fairly straightforward question, but she tried to clarify anyway. "Do his players like him? Is he nice to them?"

Kyle looked away and shrugged. "I think the girls just want to win gold balls."

Principal Hogan called them back to order for behavior modification training. As dorky as this might've been, Emily was looking forward to it. She really had no idea how to deal with misbehavior. She'd never had much experience with it, except when she was substitute teaching, and though she hadn't mentioned this during her interview, she'd pretty much let those kids do whatever they had wanted. Not her monkeys, not her circus.

But these monkeys, these would be hers.

# Chapter 4

Kyle made the fraternizing easy. About five minutes after they were released "to work on their rooms," he appeared in her doorway.

"Need any help?" he asked.

"Actually, I'm not sure how much there is to do. I mean, I'm going to put some stuff on the bulletin boards, but then what? We've got all afternoon."

"Yeah, I think this time is mostly designed for the elementary teachers, but hey, I'm not complaining." He sat down in her chair and began to swivel. "But I wanted to make sure you knew I was in the next room"—he pointed at the wall—"if you need anything."

"OK, thanks," Emily said, wondering if he was flirting.

"No really, I mean it. A kid freaks out, just come get me. I've been here five years." He leaned back in her chair, put his hands behind his head, and gave her a dazzling smile. "I'm kind of an expert at this."

She laughed, and was embarrassed at how shrill it sounded. She felt her cheeks flush, and she looked out the window. "Quite a view."

"Yep." He leaned forward, put his forearms on his knees, and looked out the window. "Most coastal towns would've turned this into condos, but not Piercehaven."

She raised an eyebrow. "Why's that?"

He shrugged. "This is a weird town. We get a few tourist types in the summer, but not many. I think maybe the long ferry ride deters them. Or maybe it's that there's not much to do when they get out here. Nowhere to stay really. Other islands have more to offer." He shrugged again and turned his gaze toward her. "I don't know really. I've lived here a long time, and I still don't understand it. It just seems panthers aren't too eager to share their island."

"A long time? I thought you said you'd only been here five years."

He smiled and looked down at his hands, which were clasped together. "I've been teaching here five years, but before that, I grew up here."

This surprised her. He just didn't seem to *fit*.

He seemed to sense her incredulity. "Yeah, I know. It doesn't make sense to me either."

"You don't seem to really like it here."

He looked at her for a beat. "Was that a question?"

She smiled sheepishly and looked out the window again. "Not really. I guess I'm just wondering why you came back?" As soon as the words left her lips, she felt guilty. "Sorry, I'm prying."

"No, that's no problem. It's a long story, but I guess I just came back because I could. I didn't do too well on the mainland." He paused. Then he slapped her desk and stood up. "But! Don't get me wrong. It's not that I don't like it here. I mean, I don't, really, but I don't *not* like it either."

She stared at him.

"Sorry, I'm overwhelming you with too much information."

"No, no, it's OK. I'm really curious. Seems like you're the perfect person to help me figure this place out."

"I'll do my best." He put his hands on his hips. "Why the big smile? Your eyes are practically twinkling."

"I just can't believe you were ever a panther."

He chuckled. "Well, I wasn't, really. I was the weird band kid. I didn't play sports. I hated it here as a kid."

"Is your family still here?"

"Oh yes. Nothing but death will drag them away. I'll let you get back to work, but if you need anything, really, I'll be bored next door, and eager to help."

Emily watched him walk away, and then looked around her empty room. *I should probably start planning.* Her head, as well as her heart, were bursting with ideas, but she knew that wasn't the same thing as laying out an organized plan.

It took her all afternoon to excavate the drawers in her new desk and the filing cabinets. Thousands upon thousands of grammar worksheets and photocopies of "The Lottery" spilled out of stacked manila folders. She figured it would be easier to start from scratch than to sort through these artifacts. She filled her recycling bin, and then filled Kyle's as well.

When she had finished gutting her classroom, she stood in the center of it with her hands on her hips. *Where on earth is the curriculum?* She planned on crafting her own lesson plans, but shouldn't there be something to get her started? A plan? An outline? A syllabus or two?

She sneezed.

"Bless you" came from the other side of the wall.

She made a mental note of the thinness of her walls. Then she sneezed again.

"Bless you more."

She headed toward Kyle's room.

He was sitting at his desk, looking down at his laptop. He looked up when she appeared in her doorway. "Finding some dust bunnies?"

"Yes. Both of the literal and metaphorical variety."

He laughed.

Her stomach fluttered. She tried to ignore it. *I don't even know if he's a believer yet. I can't go getting all smitten.* She cleared her throat. "I can't seem to find any curriculum. Is it in a secret filing cabinet somewhere?"

He laughed. "No, sorry. There probably isn't any."

She frowned. "How's that possible?"

"Well, I'm not sure there ever was one. I mean, I'm sure Alec—that's your predecessor—had a plan, but I'm not sure he had a curriculum per se. And no one around here really asks to see such a thing. I mean, we're all supposed to go by Common Core, but even that has some wiggle room—"

"Seriously?"

He crossed his arms. "Well, yeah, ideally we get to teach the standards, but often, these kids are so far behind the standards that we end up doing more remedial work. Alec was often just focused on getting the kids to read something, read *anything*, more than hewas on getting them to *distinguish satire*," he said, making air quotes around the standard. "I mean, how many of these kids are going to need satire? Don't get me wrong. I would *love* to have my students evaluating historical sources based on current evidence, but I usually don't get past a simple understanding of point of view." He paused, rubbing his jaw. "You'll see. You just meet the kids where they are, and work with what you've got."

"Why are they so behind?"

He rolled his eyes. "There just aren't enough hours in the day. The kids miss a lot of school. The only thing they really work at is apathy. None of them actually *want* to learn anything."

"None of them?"

"OK, maybe there's one per class, but not always."

"Why did he leave?"

"Who, Alec?"

She nodded.

He didn't say anything for several seconds. Then, without looking at her, he said, "The island isn't for everyone. The winters are really long, especially for a single guy—"

"Are you a single guy?"

He looked at her then, and she blushed. She hadn't meant to be so forthright.

"I am, but I go to the mainland just about every weekend."

"Even in the winter?"

"Especially in the winter."

"So is that the only reason he left? To find a woman?"

"Do you have your class schedule yet?"

She shook her head.

"Come on, let's go get it."

# Chapter 5

Emily's first period class was Freshman English.

She stood outside her classroom, greeting each student as they turned to go into her room, with a smile that she knew must look forced. She knew she had to portray a calm and confident demeanor, so she kept her hands, which were literally shaking, clasped behind her back.

She was as nervous as she'd ever been. She was also thoroughly excited. She'd never in her life been so certain that she was in the right place. Exactly where God wanted her to be.

When the bell rang, she entered the room and gently closed the door behind her. She had arranged the desks in a circle, and so a circle of eyes stared at her expectantly. Fourteen eyes. Seven students. Seven freshmen in the whole school. She slid into one of the empty desks.

"Hi, guys. My name is Miss Morse, and I am thrilled to be your new language arts teacher."

Only a few snickers.

"So, let's go around the circle, and each of you please tell me your name and one cool thing about yourself."

Aiden told her that he loved dirt bikes. That seemed normal enough.

Tyler claimed he couldn't think of anything to share.

Caleb told her he was a lobsterman. Not "my dad is a lobsterman" but "*I* am a lobsterman."

Victoria told her she was on the basketball team.

"Oh, wow! So you must be excited to finally play on the high school team!"

Victoria looked at her as if she were the stupidest person on the island.

"We can play high school sports in seventh grade here," Caleb said.

"Ah! Because we're so small?"

"We?" Tyler repeated sarcastically.

"Shut up, Tyler," Caleb said. "Yes, because we're small. We're like the second smallest high school in the state, not counting the Christian ones that have like ten kids."

Every kid laughed.

"OK, then, moving on ..." Emily looked at the next student. "What's your name?"

The get-to-know-you name game and going over the syllabus ate up the entire forty minutes of each class. By her prep period, Emily was exhausted. She closed her classroom door and fell into her chair. The door immediately opened behind her, and Kyle entered.

"How's it going?"

"You have a prep period right now too?"

"Nah, I've got kids in my room. I just ducked out to check on you. Everything OK?"

"Everything's good, I think. I mean, really good. Kids have been great."

"So, you haven't asked them to do anything yet?"

She smiled. "Right. I have not."

"OK then. Enjoy your downtime." He vanished, and she caught herself looking at his bottom as he left. This made her wonder what Bible-dashboard-guy was doing. He didn't work at the high school. Was he a lobsterman? What else did men do for work around here? Then she realized, with regret, that she didn't even know if he lived on the island. He could have been just visiting. What a tragedy that would be.

Her fifth period prep, which flew by, was followed by lunch, and she had lunch duty. Much to her delight, so did Kyle. She found him leaning against a wall with a half-eaten protein bar and a bottle of water.

She tried to look confident, for both the kids' and Kyle's benefit, as she strode across the gym to stand beside him. "Oh keeper of all island knowledge," she began, and much to her satisfaction, his eyes lit up, "can you tell me why our gym has a tiled floor?"

"Or do you mean why our cafeteria has basketball hoops?"

She nodded. "Or that, yes." She leaned back against the red wall pads and tried to look cool.

"No idea. It's always been like this. I didn't even know it was strange until I graduated. I mean, I never once gave it an ounce of thought, but I remember thinking that the Civic Center was fancy because it had hardwood floors.

"Civic Center?"

"Yeah, in Augusta, where they play the tournament games. Just because I didn't play basketball doesn't mean I didn't go to the tournament games. The whole island goes to those. It would be downright freaky to stay here during tourney time. You'd be the only one on the island."

"I doubt they empty out the nursing homes?"

He looked at her.

"What? We do have a nursing home, don't we?"

"Yes, but just one. You said, *homes*, as in plural. We don't have that many old people. And most of them do go to Augusta."

"What else don't we have?"

"Excuse me for a second."

Emily watched him walk to a table full of kids and then say a few words. One of the kids removed his earbuds, while the other kids laughed. Kyle returned to his spot along the wall.

"Aren't you going to eat?" he asked.

"I ate during my prep."

"Good thinking. So, we have lots of stuff. We've got a library, a grocery store, and a post office. We have a health clinic, with one doctor. We don't have a pharmacy, but they do have some drugs right there at the clinic. We've got a veterinarian too—"

"Any animal shelter?" she interrupted.

He shook his head. "Why? You looking to get rid of someone?"

She laughed. "No. Go on."

# PIERCEHAVEN

"So we've got a bar that serves food, a bar that doesn't serve food, and a restaurant that doesn't serve booze. We *don't* have a movie theater, bookstore, bowling alley, or Walmart."

"Do you have a church?"

He gave her a sidelong glance. "Yep. We've got one of those. Why, you're not a Bible thumper are you?"

*Well, that answers one question.*

"Only one church? On the whole island?"

He nodded, as he pointed to a milk carton someone had dropped.

"What kind of church is it?"

"I don't know. Protestant, I think."

The boy stooped to retrieve the milk carton and threw it away.

"Wow, they kind of obey you."

"Not really. It's only the first day."

# Chapter 6

The sophomore class was huge. Twelve students took up every desk she had in the room. She wheeled her own chair over and perched slightly outside the circle.

This bunch was talkative, and she didn't even get through the introductions before the bell rang.

"That's OK," she said, as they all got up and noisily gathered their things, completely ignoring her, "we'll finish this tomorrow." Some of them were out the door before she finished her sentence. Feeling a smidge scorned, she pushed her chair back to her desk. When she turned around to sit, she saw a pretty young woman standing meekly in front of her desk.

"Hi, I'm Chloe," the girl said, and held out her hand.

Emily shook it. "Nice to meet you, Chloe. Thanks for introducing yourself."

"You're welcome. And welcome to the island."

As Chloe turned to go, Emily noticed her T-shirt. "TobyMac?"

Chloe turned back toward her, wearing a huge smile. "Yeah! You a fan?"

"Indeed I am. Chloe, can I ask you an odd question?"

Chloe nodded and took a step toward her desk.

Emily leaned across it and softly asked, "Is there really only one church on the island?"

Chloe giggled and rolled her eyes. "Yes. But we meet for house church on Baker Street, if you want to come to that."

Emily was skeptical. "Is it at your house?"

"No, it's at Noah's house actually—"

"Noah?"

"Yeah, he's a junior. Wicked nice. He's in your next class, I think. Anyway, we meet in the basement of his house. But I *know* you'd be welcome to come. We invite everyone. I could draw you a map?"

"That would be great, but right now, you'd better get to your next class."

Chloe gave her another huge smile. "This is my next class. I'm in your creative writing class too! I'll go get started on your map." And with much resolve, she whirled away from Emily and returned to her desk.

Emily, knowing that teachers are never supposed to have favorites, thought maybe she'd just found hers.

There were only five students in creative writing, all upperclassmen except for Chloe, who did get to introduce herself this time, when she shared that she too was a basketball player.

"Wow!" Emily said. "It seems every female student I've had today has been a basketball player. How many girls are on the team?"

"All of them," Thomas said, and everyone laughed.

"There were twelve of us last year," Chloe explained. "There will probably be thirteen this year, as we only lost one senior and we've got two seventh graders moving up."

"I can't believe that seventh graders play against seniors," Emily said. "Don't they get trampled?"

"Well, they're *on the team*," Duke said. "That doesn't mean they actually *play*." Duke was the closest thing to a hippie that Emily had seen on the island. His long, unkempt, thick, black hair was parted so that one of his eyes was completely covered.

"At least they're on a team, dipwad," Thomas said, and everyone laughed again.

"Oh yeah, what team are you on?" Duke sneered.

"The stud-muffin team," Thomas said, which, much to Emily's surprise, everyone found funny.

In an attempt to redirect, Emily asked, "Is that why we don't have soccer teams? Because we don't have enough kids?"

Duke made a hissing sound. "We don't have soccer teams because everybody's too busy playing basketball."

An alarm sounded so deafeningly it took Emily's breath away. The kids acted as though such a thing was commonplace and stood up.

"It's just a fire drill," Chloe yelled over the noise. "Happens every first day!" She hooked her arm through Emily's and led her to the door.

Once outside in the brilliant sunshine, Emily was able to see just how tiny the school was. The entire student body took up one small corner of the parking lot. She tried to do a quick headcount, but the young ones wouldn't hold still.

"Not very many of us, are there?" Chloe asked, apparently reading Emily's mind.

"No. Do you know how many students there are?"

"I don't, but we're usually around 130."

"One hundred and thirty for the whole school?"

"Yeah, and it stays pretty steady from year to year, at least that's what they say. I don't really pay attention."

"Understandable. It's just so hard to believe that you have such a good basketball team with so few girls."

"Those few girls play together *a lot*." Chloe sounded defensive.

"I'm sorry, I didn't meant to insult you—"

"No, you didn't. It's just that, people don't understand. We start playing as soon as we can dribble, so by the time we're in high school, it's like telepathy. And we all have the same goal. We're all very motivated."

"That goal being?"

Chloe looked at her, and Emily was taken aback by the sheer innocent beauty of those eyes. "The gold ball, of course."

# Chapter 7

When Emily got to school the following Monday, Thomas and Chloe were in her classroom waiting for her.

"What are you guys doing here?" she asked, sounding a bit more aggressive than she'd meant to.

"Waiting for you," Chloe said.

"Why?"

"Because we *like* you," Chloe said slowly, as if that had been a stupid question. "And because there's really nowhere else to hang out, and because I wanted to ask you why you didn't come to church on Sunday."

Thomas moaned.

"What?" Chloe snapped.

"You didn't tell me we were going to talk about church. And besides, it's not a church. It's a lobsterman's basement."

"Whatevs. So, Emily, why didn't you come?"

Emily looked at Chloe wide-eyed. "Did you just call me by my first name?"

"Sure, we call all our teachers by their first name."

"But why?"

"Welcome to the island," Thomas said sardonically.

"No really. Why?" Emily repeated.

Chloe shrugged and looked at the floor.

"Don't be embarrassed, Chloe. I'm not angry. I just genuinely want to know why."

Thomas picked a stapler up off her desk and began to fiddle with it. "Because most of the people in this school are related. So if your aunt is the art teacher, you're probably not going to call her Mrs. Warren."

"Is your aunt the art teacher, Thomas?"

"Yep."

"OK, will you guys do me a favor?"

Chloe looked at her. "Sure?"

"Call me Miss Morse? I'm not related to any of you."

They both nodded.

"So?" Chloe asked.

"So what?"

"Why didn't you come to church?"

"I don't know. I will come. I do appreciate the invite. I just, I had a lot going on. It was my first weekend in the new place, and I was still getting settled in—"

"So you're saying you chickened out," Chloe said.

Despite herself, Emily laughed. "No, that's not what I'm saying." She sat down in her chair just as the bell rang. "Tell you what? Next Sunday, I'll go if Thomas goes."

"Ha!" Thomas said, standing up and replacing her stapler. "My grandmother would kill me. She goes to the *real* church. She'd never forgive me if I went to hang out with a bunch of Jesus freaks in a basement, instead of going to church with her."

"OK, you go to church with her, and I'll go to church with Chloe."

Thomas looked taken aback. "I'll think about it."

As Chloe and Thomas left the room, the custodian appeared in the doorway. "You mind picking up your room before you leave today?" he barked at her as the freshmen filed in.

She stared at him, speechless.

"This room was a pigsty. I don't have time to pick up after pigs."

She felt her face grow hot as she forced her jaw closed. The students all stared at her. She tried to give them a reassuring smile, but her eyes were rapidly filling with hot tears. She wanted to say something witty, to blow it off, but she didn't trust her voice not to crack.

Victoria came to her rescue. "Don't mind Larry, Miss Morse. He's a buttwad."

Emily started to correct her, but couldn't make herself speak.

Victoria sat down, continuing, "He always tries to bully new teachers. Actually, he tries to bully everyone, even kids. He hates kids. Hates everyone, I'm pretty sure."

"Well, he's been here like a hundred years," Sydney added.

"Can't you get him fired?" Tyler asked Sydney.

"What?" Sydney snapped. There couldn't possibly have been more contempt in her eyes. She obviously found Tyler to be a much lesser human being than herself.

"Well your dad's on the school board. Just go crying to him, and bam!" Tyler smacked his desk. "Syd gets what Syd wants. No more Larry."

"Shut up, Tyler! It's not like that!"

"Guys," Emily said, finally finding her voice, "let's not go down this road."

Sydney, completely ignoring Emily, swore at Tyler.

"Sydney!" Emily snapped.

"Careful, Teach," Tyler said snarkily, never taking his eyes off Sydney. "She'll get you fired too."

"That's enough, Tyler." Emily wondered how things had spiraled out of control so quickly. "Let's all take out *Lord of the Flies*."

The class groaned, but Tyler and Sydney were still glaring at each other.

Emily went through the motions of a Socratic circle, but the incident nagged at her brain, so she asked the two students to stay after class for a minute. Sydney rolled her eyes, but they both approached her desk after the bell. Tyler stood smirking, his hands in his pockets. Sydney stood with her arms crossed, a sparkly backpack slung over one shoulder.

"I'm wondering if you should both come by after school, so we can talk about what happened today—"

"Can't," Sydney proclaimed, barely letting Emily finish her sentence.

"Why not?" Emily asked.

"Basketball practice."

Emily looked out the window, as if to confirm there were still leaves on the trees. "It's September."

"Yep," Sydney said.

Emily found her confidence unnerving. The kid was only fourteen, for crying out loud.

Apparently feeling sympathetic toward Emily, Tyler, using a fake exaggerated Downeast accent, explained, "'Round here, Miss Morse, people play basketball all year 'round. From sunup to sundown. Rain, sleet, snow, fire, doesn't matter—"

"Shut up, Tyler!" Sydney interrupted.

"Sydney, that's enough!" Emily glanced up to see her room now nearly full of juniors. "Tyler, you can go. Sydney, I'll see you after school. Be here right after the bell."

"What?" Sydney shrieked. "You've got to be kidding me!"

Emily's heart pounded. She hadn't meant for this to get confrontational. "I just want to talk, that's all. Won't take long. I'll talk to your coach if that would help."

Sydney laughed humorlessly. "Milton? Like he's going to care what you say." She turned and stormed out of the room.

Watching her tiny body stomp so furiously, her sparkly backpack bouncing, would have been humorous, if Emily hadn't been so uncomfortable with the whole situation.

She took a deep breath and turned to face her juniors.

"What was that all about?" Hannah asked.

Emily shook her head. "Nothing."

# PIERCEHAVEN

"PeeWee's not going to like that," Thomas said, and the whole class laughed.

# Chapter 8

"Who's PeeWee?" Emily asked Kyle, as soon as she saw him at lunch duty.

He laughed. "Nice to see you too. Rough morning?"

She nodded expectantly.

Kyle leaned back against the gym pads, crossed his arms, and looked out at the dining adolescents. "PeeWee is Kermit Hopkins. You can see why he might let people call him PeeWee."

Emily didn't understand, and her silence apparently communicated that.

Kyle looked at her. "You know, with a first name like Kermit? But, he is a rather diminutive man. They say he used to be quite the point guard." Kyle didn't sound impressed. "Why, you haven't heard from him already, have you?"

"No, but I sort of gave his daughter a detention."

Kyle raised an eyebrow. "Sort of?"

"Well, I didn't use that word, but I asked her to come by after school, so we could talk."

"Talk about what?"

"The fact that she told a classmate to shut up, *twice*. And she swore in my classroom. Loudly." Emily watched Sydney squeeze between two other girls at one of the lunch tables.

"She won't show," Kyle said matter-of-factly.

"Is that so?"

"It is."

"Fine." Emily strode, exuding a confidence she didn't quite feel, toward Sydney's table; said, "Excuse me" to the girls sitting opposite her; and then squeezed between them, just as Sydney had done minutes before.

"Can we help you?" Sydney said.

"Well, I heard that you weren't planning to come by my room after school, so I thought we could talk now."

"What?" Sydney appeared to be genuinely confused.

"Well, I wanted to talk about your feelings, but since you plan to not show up for our appointment, I thought we could talk about them now."

There were a few nearby giggles.

"Maybe your friends would like to be part of the conversation."

Sydney's chin dipped. Every girl at the table was staring at her, except for Chloe, whose wide eyes were focused on Emily.

"I never said I wouldn't come."

"Oh, you didn't? OK, then, I must have misunderstood. Sorry for the confusion." Emily slapped the table with both hands, leaned back and looked at the girls on either side of her. "So, you heard her, girls! She'll be there. Hold her to that, will you?"

Emily managed to extricate herself from her seat without pushing off any teenager's shoulder, and then headed back toward Kyle, who was grinning foolishly.

"What was *that*?" he asked.

"Just doing some bonding."

"Not too worried about old PeeWee, are you?"

"Maybe a little," she admitted. "But I'm going to do a good job here. I don't really think the school board is going tofire me for trying to maintain classroom order." She spoke the sentence declaratively, but her raised eyebrow added a hint of question.

"Maybe not," Kyle said, which offered her no comfort.

"I'm more worried about Larry. What's up with him?"

"The custodian?"

"Yes."

Kyle grew visibly agitated. "That guy. Best thing you can do is just ignore him. He thinks he runs the school. Drives everyone nuts."

"Well, has anyone ever tried to address his behavior?"

"I spoke to Hogan about it once. He said, and I quote, 'Teachers come and go. I'm stuck with Larry.'"

Emily frowned. "What does that mean?"

"I think it means that his official position as principal is to choose the path of least resistance, and since we teachers don't have a long shelf life here, well, best to stick by the custodian."

"Well, that's bizarre."

"Welcome to the island."

The bell rang, sending a flurry back into the hallway. Thomas offered her a fist bump as he passed. She wasn't sure why, but she gratefully accepted.

Kyle leaned over her shoulder to whisper into her ear, sending a shiver up her spine.

"His stepmom's on the school board too. I think he was just saying, 'I've got your back.'"

"Oh," Emily said, watching the small crowd squeeze through the door. "Well, that was nice of him."

"Yep. Thomas is good people."

Emily was learning to love her afternoons. The sophomore class was big by comparison, but they were also a docile bunch. Of course, it could have been the time of day. Then creative writing, which she loved, took her through to the final bell. She was starting to figure out that if she could

just make it to her prep period, the rest of the day would take care of itself.

She asked the sophomores to take out their Gatsbies. They did, most of them grudgingly. One of the boys was absent, so she slid into his seat and opened her own copy, which was rife with Post-It notes and highlights, and had a spine mostly made of duct tape. She considered this the greatest American novel ever written, and felt compelled to convince these fifteen-year-olds of the same.

"MacKenzie, what did you learn about Daisy from reading this chapter?"

MacKenzie stared straight down at the closed paperback on her desk and shrugged.

Emily hadn't meant to pick on MacKenzie, hadn't started with her for any particular reason, and now wished she'd begun with someone else.

"MacKenzie?"

"What?" She still didn't look up.

Someone to Emily's left snickered, but she ignored it.

"Did you read the chapter?"

She shrugged again.

"I'll be grading this discussion, MacKenzie. It's how I evaluate whether you understood the reading, and it's how you practice your listening and speaking skills."

MacKenzie didn't respond. Nothing. Not even a shrug this time.

Emily didn't want to badger her, but she also wanted to save face with the rest of the class. So she just sat there, awkwardly staring at her student and frantically trying to decide how to proceed.

Glenn saved her, sort of. "MacKenzie's not real famous for doing her homework."

MacKenzie finally lifted her eyes, to glare at Glenn.

"This isn't homework," Emily said. She knew better than to assign homework. Her education classes had made it clear that homework was obsolete. Students didn't do it, and teachers had no recourse. If a student won't do something, and you can't make him do it, why try? "This isn't homework," she repeated, looking around the room. "This is *reading*. I only asked you to read one chapter, over a weekend. How else are you going to experience this novel if you don't read it?"

"Alec read books *to* us," Glenn said.

"Alec. So you called your previous teacher by his first name?"

"Not at first," Glenn said. "But we wore him down."

The class laughed.

Emily was suddenly quite tired. And couldn't believe it was only Monday. "So, Mr. Pratt read novels aloud to you?"

"What are novels?" Glenn asked.

The class laughed again. Someone called Glenn an idiot.

"Not novels, usually," Chloe said softly. "Mostly short stories."

Emily looked around the room. "I'm sorry, guys, but we can't let you graduate without reading some novels, especially Gatsby."

Glenn snorted. "Graduate? We're only sophomores."

"I know," Emily tried, "but you'll be seniors soon. Are you planning to start reading novels then?"

"What do you care?" Glenn said. "You won't be here." He said it without an ounce of malice, but as if it was simply an established fact, something that everyone already knew.

"You don't know that, Glenn," Chloe said. "She might stick around."

"Really? What's so different about this one?" Glenn said.

"I dunno. I think she kind of likes us." Chloe gave Emily a small smile, which Emily felt as a tangible warmth in her chest.

Emily took a deep breath. "I'll be honest with you guys. I plan to stay here for a very, very long time. I plan to teach Gatsby to your children. Now, you be honest with me. I won't hold it against any of you. Just tell the truth. Raise your hand if you read Chapter One."

One hand crept up. Chloe's.

Sydney did show up after school, but she made Emily wait first. She came nonchalantly strolling in fifteen minutes after the final bell. Then she plopped down in a desk and stared at Emily expectantly.

Emily dragged another desk to hers and sat down opposite her. She leaned back and, remembering her training, resisted the urge to cross her arms. "How are you doing, Sydney?"

Sydney scowled. "Fine."

"Good to hear it. I hope that's true. Now, I wanted to speak with you about what happened with Tyler today. How do you think he felt after interacting with you?"

"What?" There was that utter confusion again.

"You told him to shut up. And you swore at him. How do you think that made him feel?"

"It's *Tyler*. I don't really care how it made him feel."

"And why's that?"

Sydney looked dumbfounded. "I don't know. Look, I won't do it again. Can I go?"

"Well, how do *you* feel when someone tells you to shut up?"

"No one tells me that."

Emily took a deep breath. "How *would* you feel if someone *did* tell you to shut up?"

"No one would."

Every cell in Emily's body wanted to give up, but she persisted. "Sydney, how we treat others *matters*. I think, deep down, you know this."

Sydney leaned forward. "Miss Morse, I don't think you have any idea how high school *works*."

"OK. Well, why don't you tell me?"

She rolled her eyes. "Guys like Tyler, they need to be put in their place. He's an idiot. I've

59

been dealing with him since preschool. I know how to handle him. It's not a big deal."

Emily didn't know where to go from there. After an awkward pause, she went with, "I don't think we ever know how 'big a deal' something is for someone else. I need for you to not tell anyone to 'shut up' in my classroom, and to not swear at anyone. Can you do that for me?"

"Whatevs."

"Can you do that?" Emily repeated.

"Fine."

# Chapter 9

It was the longest week of Emily's life, but she managed to get the first few chapters of *The Great Gatsby* read aloud to her sophomores, and even managed to get a few of them to comment on the story. She had to bribe them with the promise of watching the movie when it was all over. *You'll be sorry,* she thought. *It's quite terrible.*

On Friday afternoon, she collapsed into Kyle's chair. "How do you get them to do anything?"

Kyle laughed. "I rarely do. What makes you ask?"

"I told them we were going to do a Gatsby skit, you know, act out a chapter. I'm trying to get them engaged, but all but one of them refused to participate."

"Which one?"

"Which one what?"

"Which one didn't refuse to participate?"

"Oh. Chloe."

Kyle raised an eyebrow.

"You're surprised? That kid's a saint."

"She's a good kid, yes." He stooped to pick up some trash. "But she's not usually one to go against the tide. She must have taken a liking to you."

Emily figured it was probably the TobyMac connection, or maybe even the Jesus connection, but she didn't say that. "So what? I just keep reading to them?"

Kyle bent over to peel something off the leg of a desk. "I'd say, if they're actually listening to you reading, then yes. I'd say you're getting quite a lot accomplished if that's the case. Even if some of them are tuning you out. Most of them aren't, right?"

"True. Most of them aren't. When I ask questions, they usually know the answers. But seriously? This is high school!"

"No. This is Piercehaven."

"I know, I know, welcome to the island. What happens when I ask them to actually write something?"

Kyle guffawed. "Just don't."

Emily chewed her lip for a minute, thoughtfully, watching him coil up an extension cord. "Do you ever fail anyone?"

"I wouldn't if I were you."

"That's not what I asked."

"No, but it's what you were thinking. You can fail them, but then they're just in your classroom again next year. And no one blames the kid who fails. It will be your fault. You'll be the one who failed. And for heaven's sake, don't fail a basketball player, whatever you do. The wrath of the entire island will rain down on your head."

"Speaking of basketball, they really practice all year round?"

Kyle scowled. "No. Who told you that?"

"Sydney. On Monday. Said she had practice."

"No, that's against MPA rules. They have pickup games, which the seniors supervise, and maybe they do drills or something, but I doubt it. Either way, it's not an official practice."

"But are they expected to go?"

Kyle looked at her. "Probably."

She decided she needed to change the subject, for her own sanity. "So, what do you have planned for the weekend?"

"I'm going to the mainland. Want to come?"

The question startled her. Go where? "The mainland" was a fairly vague destination. "What do you do there?"

"I go to bookstores. And bars. Maybe see a movie. Try to find a live band or two."

"Where do you stay?"

"Wherever."

*Well, that was ambiguous.* "Well thanks for the invite—"

He snickered, making her wonder if the invite had even been sincere.

"—but I think I'm getting a kitten this weekend, so I probably shouldn't leave it alone. I also want to finish the Ted Dekker series I'm reading."

"Who on earth is Ted Dekker? And a kitten? Do your hosts know that?"

"My hosts? You mean my landlords?"

"You mean you pay rent?"

Emily felt a prickling sensation on her neck. She realized, for the first time, that she didn't necessarily want everyone to know that she was living in that house for free.

Kyle must have sensed her uneasiness. "Don't be offended. 'Host' is an island word. I didn't mean anything by it."

"Did Alec live there before me?"

"He sure did. Along with the girl before him, and the guy before that."

"And they each only lasted one year?"

Kyle nodded. "So, a kitten?"

"Well, I was talking about wanting a dog, and MacKenzie Ginn said she had some kittens she had to get rid of. I figured that was

64

better than nothing, and I can still get a dog. And yes, I've checked with my *hosts*, and they're fine with it."

"You know, come to the mainland with me, and we could go dog shopping."

Emily really did want a dog. That part of the offer was tempting. But she really didn't want to go to the mainland with Kyle. She couldn't even put a finger on the source of her hesitation. The long ferry ride? Maybe. The uncertainty of where they would stay? Most likely. The probable alcohol consumption? Probably.

"You know I don't drink, right?"

"Why would I know that?"

"Sorry. Didn't mean for it to come out like that. Just wanted to tell you, I don't drink. So. There. Now you know."

"Now I know."

# Chapter 10

MacKenzie showed up on Emily's doorstep on Saturday morning. *Well this is a bit familial.* Emily shuffled to the door, trying to smooth down her hair as she went. She was still in a bathrobe.

"Hi, MacKenzie," she said, trying to sound cheery, and then she saw the small balls of fur in MacKenzie's arms, and did feel a bit cheered.

As Emily looked around her small yard to see if MacKenzie was alone, MacKenzie stepped inside uninvited. Fairly certain this was inappropriate, Emily left the front door standing open.

"I figured you might want to pick," MacKenzie said, and tried to hand her three kittens at the same time.

Only one of them meowed, complaining about the attempted transfer.

"Can I just hold one for now?" Emily asked, a tad overwhelmed. She reached out and took the gray tabby out of MacKenzie's arms, knowing as soon as she touched her that this cat would be hers, and that she would name her Daisy Buchanan. She flipped her over to verify her femaleness, but she still wasn't sure, and Daisy made it clear she wasn't having any of this. Emily rubbed her cheek against the top of Daisy's head, and caught MacKenzie staring at her. "This is so nice of you, MacKenzie. I really appreciate it."

"Do you want to take more than one?" MacKenzie said, her eyes wide with hope.

"I'd better not."

MacKenzie's eyes filled with tears as she tucked the remaining kittens under her chin.

Emily felt panic rising in her throat. "Are you OK, MacKenzie?"

She nodded, and the tears began to fall from her eyes, which refused to rise to meet Emily's.

"What is it, sweetie?" Emily put a hand on her shoulder, and MacKenzie jerked away, but the reflex was so subtle that Emily quickly convinced herself she had imagined it. Nevertheless, her hand dropped.

MacKenzie sniffed and rolled her eyes. "It's no big deal, really. My dad's just super mad that our cat got pregnant in the first place, so he won't let us keep any of the kittens. He says he's going to get rid of them if I don't find them a home, and I know what that means." She forced out these last few words quickly, and a sob followed.

"Do you want to sit down?" Emily asked, motioning toward the couch.

MacKenzie didn't answer, just collapsed on it.

"I would take more," Emily said, "but this isn't my house. I don't think—"

"Lauren and Mike?" MacKenzie's head jerked up, her eyes wide with hope. "If that's the reason, they totally won't care. My aunt Lauren loves cats, and Mike won't care. He's wicked nice. They're both wicked nice."

"Your aunt?" *Shoot.*

"Yeah. Lauren is my mom's sister. They're wicked close. I could call her and ask her, if you want."

Emily didn't know what to say. "Maybe, if she loves cats, she would take one?"

"She already has. We started with four. Do you want me to call her?"

Emily hesitated. She had no idea where to go with this. She felt it was too late to try to come up with another excuse, but she also didn't want to call her sort-of-landlords, who also happened to be school board members, and ask if she could adopt three cats, only hours after they'd told her she could have *one*. "Are they both school board members?"

"What?"

"Your aunt and uncle. They're *both* on the school board?"

"Yeah. So what?"

"How many people are on the school board?"

"How should I know?"

"Sorry, I just thought it was strange that two married people both got elected to the school board."

"They're not married."

"Oh."

It was so obvious that MacKenzie didn't care about the school board. But at least she wasn't crying anymore. "So you want me to call them?"

"No, I will," Emily said, because she couldn't think of any other course of action. She crossed the room to the phone, and dialed.

A female voice answered.

"Lauren?"

"Yes?"

"This is Emily Morse." She hated that her voice sounded embarrassed, but this whole situation was embarrassing. She wasn't even wearing a bra, and she had a student on her couch.

"Yes! Good morning, Emily."

"Good morning. I, uh, have a situation here. I have your niece, MacKenzie, here, and she's pretty upset. She wants me to adopt all three of her remaining kittens, because I guess they're in danger?" She realized she wasn't making much sense, so she began to talk faster. "I don't feel comfortable asking you if I can have three cats, after only living here for three weeks, and you've been so generous, and I'm so grateful, I didn't even want to ask, but I also don't want to break MacKenzie's heart—"

"You're so sweet. I've been hearing good things about you at that school!"

"You have?" Emily realized, too late, that she should have worked harder to keep the shock out of her voice.

"Tell you what. Do you *want* three kittens?"

Emily looked down at the one kitten clutched to her chest. "Well, not really, but I also don't want them to die."

"Well, you tell MacKenzie, if you're willing to take two, then I'll take another one, and then no kittens have to die today."

"That sounds like a deal. Thanks so much, Lauren."

"You bet. You keep up the good work in that classroom. MacKenzie won't admit it, but she's really enjoying that book you're reading to them."

"Well, that's great," Emily said, because she didn't know what else to say. She said goodbye, hung up the phone, and looked at the sophomore sitting hopefully on her couch. "Lauren says she'll take one more, and I'll take the other one."

"Awesome!" MacKenzie cried. "Which one do you want?"

"I don't know. Which one do you think I should have?"

She didn't even hesitate. She held a squealing orange tabby out toward Emily, who hastily took it. "This one," MacKenzie declared. "You can name him Nick Carraway."

Emily's head snapped up to look at MacKenzie. Had she said the name Daisy aloud? She was pretty sure she hadn't.

# Chapter 11

Emily decided it was time to go to church. Not forsaking our own assembling together and all that.

As she sipped her morning coffee, she dug around till she found the map Chloe had drawn her, and then tried to make sense of it. When she thought she had at least figured out where she was on the map, she headed up the spiral staircase to get dressed.

But she had no idea what to wear to an island basement house church meeting. After a bit of ado, she decided on one of her tried and true church dresses. Three-quarter-length-sleeves, hem just below the knee, with black pumps and a string of pearls. She checked herself in the mirror and thought, *Not bad*.

She was *so* overdressed.

But no one seemed to notice.

The twenty-two people crammed into the modest basement made her feel like a long-lost family member who had just decided to come home. Noah gave her a big welcome wave, not seeming to feel the least bit awkward having his new teacher in his cellar. Chloe was positively beaming, especially when she introduced Emily to her Uncle James. When the man turned around to face Emily, she gasped, and then immediately wished she hadn't. She rapidly stuck out her hand to make up for her faux pas, but she could feel her face flushing.

Bible-dashboard-guy smiled, graciously ignoring her unreasonably awkward social behavior, and shook her hand. "Nice to meet you, Emily. Welcome to our little church."

"It's nice to meet you too," she said, and then stood there staring up at him, smiling. He was far more handsome up close. She wanted to keep him talking. How could she keep him talking? "So you live on the island?" She wanted to die. Of course he lived on the island. No one would catch a ferry to go to a basement church.

He didn't even blink. "Born and raised."

"What do you do for work?"

"I fish."

She wasn't sure if he meant lobster or actual fish, but she thought probably lobster. She wished she'd paid more attention to the kids' lobster banter—she didn't even know the language yet. "That's nice." She wished a giant hole would open in the floor beneath her feet and suck her in.

He smiled.

"So why a house church?" she asked. She meant, *Why do you guys have church in a basement? Can't you find a church building? Where did you all come from?* But all those words seemed so far away, lost somewhere between her brain and her lips.

He seemed, somehow, to know exactly what she was asking. "Well, a few years ago, I just really felt God telling me I had to do something here on the island. There was a spattering of believers, but we were really disconnected. Some of us were going to the established church on the island, but most of us weren't. No disrespect to that group of people—they're a good bunch of people, but they don't seem to focus on Jesus much there. So anyway, I wanted to help people focus on Jesus. We started out in my house, but it is tiny, and we quickly outgrew it. So Abe here"—he nodded at a man near the front of the room, a man she assumed to be Noah's father—"and his wife Lily, she's around here somewhere, they welcomed us into their home, and here we are."

"You're the pastor?" she said, sounding so incredulous it came out mightily impolite.

He didn't seem offended. "No. We don't really have a pastor. We certainly have leaders, who just sort of took that role organically, and I suppose I'm one of those, but I'm no pastor." He leaned closer to her. "Not really into public speaking." He looked around the room and laughed. "Though I suppose this isn't very public."

She followed his gaze around the room, and finally started to relax. A little.

"Oh look,"—he touched her elbow. *Oh my word, he just touched my elbow!*—"I think we're going to get started. Let's find a seat."

She followed him to the second row and then shakily sat beside him. She knew she was grinning like a lunatic, but all self-control seemed to have fled the scene.

The man named Abe welcomed them and then started to pray.

Emily bowed her head and closed her eyes, and then physically jumped when Chloe leaned forward to whisper something in her ear. "Cute, isn't he?"

Emily's cheeks got hot. Suddenly, she was so overwhelmed with gratitude she thought her chest might crack. And as Abe prayed, Emily silently thanked God—for Chloe, for

## PIERCEHAVEN

James, for her new job, for her new kittens, for her new home, for the island.

# Chapter 12

Monday morning found Chloe and Thomas waiting at Emily's desk again.

"Good morning," Emily sang.

"Well aren't we perky today?" Thomas said with a smirk.

"What's not to be perky about?" Emily said.

"Don't try to deny it. Chloe already filled me in."

Emily looked at Chloe. "Filled you in about what?"

"Oh stop it, Em—" She stopped herself. "Miss Morse. I saw him talking to you after church. Did he ask you out? Did he?"

Emily felt her face growing red again. And even though she knew she shouldn't be acting like a teenager, she was feeling like one.

Chloe squealed. "He did, didn't he?" She clapped her hands and looked at Thomas. "I told you so!"

"Chloe, is that why you invited me to church, to play matchmaker?"

"No! But I mean, I want you to like him. Because I want you to stay. And you do like him, don't you?"

"I don't even know him yet." She sat down and opened her plan book, even though she didn't need to.

"Fine. Be that way. So when's your first date?"

Emily sighed. "Thursday."

Chloe squealed again.

Thomas clapped his hand over an ear. "Enough, Chloe!" He swore.

Emily raised an eyebrow at him.

"Sorry, Miss Morse, but she sounds like a hyena in heat."

"Did *you* go to church this weekend? With your grandmother?"

Thomas smiled evasively.

"Wasn't that part of the deal?"

The bell rang, and both students stood up. Thomas offered Emily another fist bump, which she accepted. "I've never heard a bad word about James Gagnon. I hope it works out. I want you to stay too."

"Thanks, Thomas," she said, wondering why students thought one had to be romantically involved to stay on the island. Then she figured they were just observing the patterns around them.

She found Kyle in his usual lunch duty spot, leaning against the gym pads, eating his usual protein bar.

"Hey!" he said. "Hadn't seen you yet today."

"Yeah, I didn't come in any too early."

"Not a morning person?"

"I try …" She giggled. "But no, not really. Hey, what can you tell me about James Gagnon?"

Kyle's head snapped toward her. "Why?"

"Because I met him this weekend, and he asked me out."

Kyle's jaw clenched and he looked away from her. "That right?"

She felt guilty, and didn't know why. Had she missed some signal from Kyle? They were coworkers, right? Nothing else had been developing? She sure hadn't meant for there to be. "Are you all right?"

"Yeah, of course. Just hungover. So, James Gagnon. He's all right, I guess. Was a big basketball legend and all. Now he's a fisherman. Just like everyone else."

"You don't like him."

"I didn't say that."

"You didn't have to. Why don't you like him?"

"I don't not like him, Emily. I hardly know the guy anymore."

"Anymore? So you used to know him?"

"Yeah. This is Piercehaven. Everybody knows everybody."

She waited for him to say more.

He obliged. "We went to school together. But I told you. I was the weird band kid. We didn't hang out or anything." He looked at her, but his eyes were missing their usual spark. "So yeah, go out with him. Maybe we can double date sometime."

Her eyebrows flew up. "Yeah? That'd be great. You seeing someone?"

He smiled at her, but there was no joy in it. "Sure. I'm seeing several someones." Then he walked off toward a table full of boys who seemed on the verge of fisticuffs.


She met James Thursday night at the bar that served food. He beat her there, and rose to greet her when she approached. He gave her a chaste kiss on the cheek and pulled out her chair. *Oh, I am so loving this.*

She was too nervous to look at him, so she stared at her menu. "I'm not saying I was going to order lobster, but isn't it a little strange that it's not on the menu?"

He didn't answer her at first, and the long silence forced her to glance up at him.

When she did, he said, "I don't think either of the restaurants on the island serves lobster."

"Don't people eat lobster here?"

"Sure, but they don't want to buy it. They want to pull it out of their own traps, or, if they don't have their own traps, they want to get it from Uncle Bill. Worst case scenario, they buy it from the co-op. But I doubt any of them would pay for it in a restaurant. Islanders go to restaurants to eat steak." He spoke all of this in one breath.

It occurred to her then that James was actually nervous. This made her happy.

He continued, "I myself don't care if I ever eat it again. Had enough of it growing up."

The server came and they both gave their orders. Beef all around. After the pleasantries, Emily tried to regain the thread of conversation.

"Your father was a lobsterman too?"

"Yep. I'm fourth generation."

"Wow, so you are island through and through."

He looked at her, his gaze so intense it unnerved her. She didn't know if she'd been harboring the idea that he might someday leave the island with her, but if so, that idea had just sailed off on its own.

"So what do you do for fun?" he asked, and she tried not to notice the abrupt transition.

"I read."

"That's it?"

"Mostly. I mean, I was really involved in my church back home, so that took up a lot of my free time."

"What did you do in church?"

"I helped with children's ministry. We had a fairly big one. I was there at least three nights a week."

He whistled. "We don't have a children's ministry."

She smiled. "I can see how that might happen."

"We talked about vacation Bible school this past summer, but we were never really able to get it together." He looked at her expectantly.

"What?"

"Want to start a children's ministry here? I'll help."

She didn't answer at first. Then, "I'm not sure how that would fly with my job."

The look he gave her made her instantly regret even thinking the thought.

"I know, I know," she said, trying to get out of the conversational hole, "my reward is in heaven, and if they fire me for helping children, then that would actually be a blessing."

He just stared at her.

"Well, wasn't that what you were thinking?"

"Something like that."

"It's not that I'm valuing my job over Jesus, it's just that, well, I *just* got the job. Shouldn't I keep it for a while before making waves? Maybe wait until I've got a continuing contract at least?"

He looked surprised. "You mean you plan to stay here? For years?"

She looked around the room and then back at him. "Yeah. I think so. Why not?"

He nodded thoughtfully. "You haven't seen a Piercehaven winter yet."

She found this incredibly patronizing. She'd been a Mainer all her life. "No, but I've seen plenty of Plainfield winters. Can't be much worse than that."

"Oh, but it can. It can be so, so much worse."

This annoyed her so much she wanted to leave the table, no matter how handsome he was.

He seemed to sense this, and tried to change course. "Do you know why they call it

Plainfield? Isn't it right in the middle of the mountains?"

"No," she said, looking down at her placemat. "It's at the foot of the mountains. It's the last flat land for a long time. Just a big, plain field before the exciting mountains"—she looked up at him—"where the winters are especially brutal."

After dinner, James offered to give her a tour of the town. This excited her. She wanted to ride around with him in his truck. As soon as she climbed in, she looked for the Bible on the dashboard. It wasn't there. She resisted the urge to check the glovebox.

He drove through what passed for a downtown, which was about eight businesses side by side. He pointed out each one and named it, even though the signs were clearly visible. She still enjoyed the narration. His voice was deep, calm, and soothing.

Then he drove out of town, showed her the island mansion, where someone rich lived, though they were only there in the summer. The rest of the time, only employees stayed there, keeping the place up.

He drove by the dump and pointed out the swap shack.

"What's a swap shack?"

"Well … if you bring junk to the dump that's a little too good to throw away, you can put it in the swap shack. Then you paw through everything, see what junk other people have left, and take different junk home. You don't want to go in the winter, though. It's not heated."

Emily wasn't sure she wanted to go at all.

"There's usually a lot of books in there."

She changed her mind.

The road brought them back into the more populated area of the island, and James pointed to a mustard-colored ranch. "That's where the Sheriff lives. He's in his office during the day, but if you ever need him after hours, that's where he'll be, right there propped up in front of the TV."

"Don't they have a deputy cover the office after hours?"

James laughed. "We don't have any deputies. Actually, we do. The Sheriff isn't really a Sheriff. We just call him that because he's all we have. He's actually a deputy of the County Sheriff. But don't call him Deputy. He likes to be called Sheriff."

"Is it an elected position?"

"Yep, but no one ever runs against him."

"Happy Monday!" Kyle was standing outside his room, by his door, where she'd never seen him before. "How did your date go?"

She didn't really want to stop to chat. Her bags were heavy, and she wanted to get to her room so she could spend a few minutes with Chloe and Thomas before the bell rang. Not because she had anything in particular to talk about, but because she just really liked their company. "It was OK," she said, not slowing her pace.

"Ah, trouble in paradise," he said with a smirk.

She stopped then and turned halfway back to him. "No, there isn't. I like James. He seems really nice."

"Nice," Kyle muttered. "That's a word I always associate with passion." He ducked back into his room before she could reply.

And she went into hers.

"Did he kiss you?" Thomas asked, before she'd even set her bags down.

She tried to glare at him, but she was amused. "None of your business."

He *had* kissed her, on the cheek, again, a little less chaste this time, but still disappointing. And she had smiled awkwardly and said, "Let's do this again sometime," and then she had gotten into her car and driven away.

Thomas was staring at her, as if trying to read her mind. Then, apparently, he succeeded. "He *did* kiss you!" he declared. "Nice work, Chloe!" He gave Chloe a fist bump, and Emily marveled at how self-satisfied they both looked. She also marveled at how much she loved these two children.

# Chapter 13

Time was a different creature on Piercehaven. Islanders joked about "island time," which generally meant that no one really worried about punctuality; businesses opened and closed when they wanted to, but there was more to it than that. It seemed as though, on the island, time actually passed more slowly than everywhere else, as if the hands on the clock were themselves on island time, and in no hurry to get to the next minute, the next hour.

As the leaves slowly lost their green and drifted to an increasingly colder ground, Emily could feel the days getting shorter, and with that, the general pace of the island slowed, as if everyone was getting ready to hunker down for a big storm. Her sophomores did manage to finish Gatsby, did understand it, did watch the movie, did hate it, and did start *The Honk and Holler Opening Soon*, which Emily read aloud to them every day.

She had settled into a routine, and even though she liked this routine, getting up early, loving on students and kittens, then reading herself to sleep, she couldn't help but find the whole thing monotonous. And this feeling led to immediate guilt. She had a real job. She had a beautiful home (for free). She loved her students. They seemed to love her. What more could she want?

Well, she wanted James, and he certainly wasn't in any hurry. They went out once a week, and she enjoyed her time spent with him, but the relationship didn't seem to be progressing any, if it even *was* a relationship. He hadn't said so. He hadn't spoken of any sort of future. And he hadn't even kissed her on the lips yet. She was getting impatient.

It wasn't basketball season yet, but people were certainly gearing up. And what Kyle had told her about no official practices was at least partly a crock. The kids played some of their pickup games on the outside court, and Emily had seen Milton Darling out there more than a few times. Not every time, but still.

Mid-October, Milton approached her about Jasmine's grade. He had looked at her grades online, and seen that she was currently getting a C in AP English.

Just the way he entered her room annoyed her. He walked in as if he *owned* the room. Then he actually sat on her desk, well, at least, half-sat on it, with one leg still on the floor, so he was perched above her and looking down at her. She self-consciously pulled up the front of her blouse.

"You're giving Jazzy a C?"

She blinked, taking a second to realize that Jazzy meant Jasmine. "Well, I'm not *giving* her anything. She'll receive the grade she's earned—"

"Well the quarter ends in two weeks. Don't you think you should have talked to me about this?"

She laughed. She couldn't help it.

His jaw clenched.

Her smile fell away. "Why would I talk to you about it?"

"Because I'm the coach, and everyone knows we make sure basketball players don't flunk!" His sentence grew louder with each word, his body rising up to a standing position. He ended in a crescendo with his hands on his hips.

Kyle appeared in the doorway, but Emily didn't look at him. She didn't want to look away from Milton. "She's not flunking. If she

90

was, then *she* should talk to you about it. I don't really give a hoot about basketball."

"Hey!" Kyle said, approaching the scene with quick steps. He gave Milton a good-ol'-boy slap on the shoulder. "Emily here is still figuring things out. Why don't you cut her some slack, OK?"

Milton glared at him.

Kyle lowered his voice. "I'll take care of it, OK? Trust me. She's good people. We don't want to chase her off. She'll work with you."

Milton gave Emily another glare and then stomped off like a toddler mid-tantrum.

"Did that really just happen?" she asked Kyle when he was gone.

"Yep, and it will happen again if you don't get her up to a B."

"Get her up? Are you hearing yourself? She's in *Advanced Placement* English! It's hard! And she's not doing any of the work! She's lucky to have a C right now."

Kyle shook his head slowly. "Trust me, you don't want to do this."

"Do what? So the kid has to sit out for a quarter. Wouldn't that be a valuable lesson?"

Kyle sighed. "Will you please listen to me?" He dragged a kid's desk over to hers and sat down. "That's not the way it would happen. Here's what would happen. Milton will go to the parents. The parents will go to the principal. And she'll either be yanked from your class or you'll be fired. Or both. No way this ends with the starting center sitting out for a quarter. Not in a million years."

"So what? I'm just supposed to fabricate grades?"

"No. You're supposed to help them be successful. If that means simplifying the course materials, then so be it."

"I can't *simplify* it, Kyle. It's *AP*."

"OK then. If I can't convince you, fine. But don't say I didn't warn you."

They stared at each other for a long minute. Then Kyle asked, "You like teaching here?"

"Of course. I love it."

He looked skeptical.

"OK, well, I love the kids."

He nodded. "And you don't mind living on the island?"

"No, it's beautiful. And if you say anything ominous about winter, we're done here."

He chuckled. "And you like James Gagnon?"

She glared at him, thinking, *Did you really just bring James into this?*

He nodded again. "Then you won't flunk Jasmine Lane. She's a solid ten points per game, and twice that many rebounds." He stood up. "You can find a way to do it that's still ethical. Figure it out." He turned to go.

"I thought you didn't even care about basketball?" she called after him.

"I don't," he said, without turning around.

# Chapter 14

Emily gave her AP students a ridiculously easy pop quiz, and then she gave it extra weight in the grade book. Everyone in the class got hundreds, except for Jazzy, who got a C.

Emily was furious. She asked her to stay after class.

"I was wondering if you might want to do an extra credit project?"

"No, why?"

"I thought you might want to get your C up to a B?" Emily answered, trying to appear gracious and not as annoyed as she truly felt.

"Milton said you were going to take care of that."

Grace flew out the window. "This *is* me taking care of it, Jasmine. I can't just give you a grade. That wouldn't be fair to the other students who are earning theirs. If you want a B, you'll have to do something extra."

"Like what?"

"I've printed out a list of classic novels." She handed her a sheet of paper. "You need to pick one and read it."

"Then what?"

"Then I'll let you know."

She rolled her eyes and slid out of the room.

One week later, Emily gave her AP students time to start on another assignment and called Jasmine to her desk.

"Have a seat. Let's discuss your book."

"I'm not finished yet."

"Well, let's discuss what you've read so far."

The look on Jasmine's face said all Emily needed to know.

"You haven't started yet?"

Jasmine stared at her obstinately.

"You do realize that I *can* fail you, right? Milton can't actually control your English grade."

"You'll get fired if you fail me."

Emily felt her face get hot. She leaned closer to Jasmine and without thinking first, said, "You think you're stubborn? You have no idea how stubborn I can be. And maybe I'll just decide that it's worth it? Maybe I'll sacrifice this job just to see you sit out for an entire quarter of basketball. I have done stranger things for lesser causes. Do you really want to test me?"

The dawning fear in Jasmine's eyes brought Emily tremendous satisfaction.

"That book is due one week from today. Or we'll find out who is the most stubborn."

One week later, Jasmine sat in the chair beside Emily's desk.

Emily began asking her questions about *The Old Man and the Sea*. Jasmine answered the first few correctly, giving Emily hope that this situation might actually end on a positive note. But when Emily asked her what the blood and the sharks represented, Jasmine's face registered horror, as if she'd never heard of such a thing.

"Jasmine, give me your book."

"What?"

"Hand me *The Old Man and the Sea*. I want to see it."

"I already took it back to the library."

"OK, great, I'm going to go check with the librarian and see if you ever checked it out." Emily stood.

"No, wait!"

Emily looked at her expectantly.

"Give me one more chance," she begged.

Suddenly, Emily was very tired. "I want a written summary on my desk in two days. This is your last chance."


Emily explained the entire situation to James over dinner. She didn't mention Jasmine's name, but she didn't need to. James seemed to know exactly whom she was talking about.

He didn't respond at first, just sat there, looking thoughtful.

Finally, he said, "I see where you're coming from, but you've got to choose your battles, Emily."

"I know that. And I think I want to choose this one."

James shook his head somberly. "You won't win this one. Instead, I would encourage you to never let yourself get into this scenario again."

"Are you telling me to never give a basketball player a C?"

"That's not what I'm telling you. She probably never should have been in AP English in the first place, and that happened before you got here. But you can keep it from happening again, now that you know all the kids. And next time something like this happens, try to get the resource room involved immediately. Then it's off your plate and onto theirs."

She nodded, feeling resigned. "How'd you get to be so wise?"

"I'm not wise. I just know how the island works."

The next day, Jasmine laid a book report on Emily's desk.

Initially, Emily was impressed with how well-written it was, but then she got suspicious. She Googled two adjacent sentences and instantly learned that Jasmine had cut and pasted from SparkNotes. She hadn't even bothered to paraphrase any of it.

Her laziness was remarkable. *She must think I'm stupid*, Emily thought, but then she opened her laptop, double-clicked the online gradebook, and bumped Jasmine's grade up to a B.

# Chapter 15

November 16 was the first official day of basketball season, and there was a new energy in the air. Kids weren't talking about basketball any more than usual, but most of the kids just seemed happier all of a sudden. *Most* of the kids. Not Duke. Not Thomas. So Emily's seventh period creative writing class was still on an even keel.

Until Hailey read her persona poem aloud, which was written from the point of view of a basketball hoop.

Duke groaned.

Emily tried to shush him, but it was too late.

"What?" Hailey snapped defensively.

"*What?* You seriously need to ask? The teacher says you can write from the perspective of literally anything or anyone in the universe, and you pick a basketball hoop?"

Hailey looked at Emily, waiting for her to intervene.

"You're right, Duke. She could write about anything, and this is what she chose. You don't have to like it. It's art, which is always subjective. But you do have to respect it, and respect Hailey."

Duke rolled his eyes. "I do respect Hailey. She's one of the good ones, but you don't understand, Miss Morse. This is only the first day. Soon it's all we'll hear about. Scores and Heal points will be announced over the intercom. Box scores will be taped to lockers. Everyone will wear jerseys to school, but only on game days, because they don't even come on non-game days, 'cause they're oh so tired."

"That's not true," Hailey snapped. "I always come to school."

"I know *you* do, but like I said"—he looked around the room as if for affirmation—"you're one of the good ones. You can't tell me that your teammates don't take advantage of the situation."

Emily didn't know what to say, and the room was pregnant with the awkward silence.

"He has a point," Thomas added.

"You're just jealous," Hailey said, though it was unclear whom she was speaking to.

Duke assumed it was him. "I am *not* jealous. I have no desire to be part of the nightmare you're living in."

"The nightmare that's already getting me recruited by colleges?"

Duke snorted. "Yeah right. Like you're going to college."

"Duke!" Emily sprang to life. "That's enough out of you!"

"Sorry," Duke said to Emily, noticeably not Hailey, "but these so-called athletes *never* play in college. They don't even go to college. Or if they do, they come back after one semester with their tail between their legs. This is a Class D school. It's like being a superstar in a mud puddle."

Thomas laughed.

"Thomas!" Chloe scolded.

"You know what," Emily declared, desperate to regain some semblance of control, "everyone open your laptops. I want you to write an essay—"

"An essay?" Thomas whined. "But this is *creative* writing!"

"OK fine, it can be a poem. A poem or essay about the following topic ..." She typed "Basketball is/isn't good for this island" on her laptop, and the words appeared on the interactive board. "You choose a stance and then defend it. At least fifty lines or five hundred words. Ready, go."

They groaned, but they opened their laptops and the room filled with the clicks of keys, some clicks more emphatic than others.

Coach Milton Darling met Emily at the door the next morning. "You told your students to write an essay about how basketball isn't good for this island?" By the time he finished his accusation, his face was only inches from hers.

She would look back on this moment and wistfully think how easy it would have been to say, "Get out of my face" and keep on walking. But in that moment, she was intimidated, and frozen.

"Well?" he prodded.

"You don't have the whole story—"

"I don't need the whole story. Stop messing with my basketball players. I'm not going to tell you again." He turned and swaggered toward the gym.

When she got to her classroom, she was crying.

"What's wrong?" Chloe and Thomas asked at the same time.

She shook her head. "Just teacher junk. I'll be fine."

"Did James break up with you?" Thomas asked.

This brought on a whole new onslaught of tears. How could he break up with her if she wasn't even his girlfriend? She suddenly longed for him. She could tell him about what had just happened, and surely he'd have good advice.

"No," she said to Thomas. "He sure didn't."

"Can I pray over you?" Chloe asked softly.

"Oh, I am so out of here," Thomas said, but he didn't move.

Emily smiled. "Actually, that *would* help, if you're comfortable doing so."

"Of course!" Chloe popped up out of her chair, came around Emily's desk, and placed a gentle hand on her teacher's shoulder. They both bowed their heads, and Thomas stared at them. "Father, I ask to reach into this situation right now. I don't know what's going on, but you do. Please touch Miss Morse's heart right now and give her comfort and peace, so that she can focus on her students today. In Jesus' name I pray, amen."

"Amen," Emily repeated. She raised her head to meet Thomas's eyes, and what she saw there was mostly curiosity. "You know, Thomas, it's not all just a bunch of bunk. Jesus is very real, and he's involved in all aspects of our lives. If you ever have any questions, talk to Chloe or me, OK?"

The bell rang, giving Thomas a chance to escape, but he didn't take it. "You really believe it's all true, don't you?"

Emily nodded. "It *is* all true."

Chloe's prayer worked wonders, and by lunch, Emily was in better spirits than she'd been in for weeks. Not only did she have a plan, she fully believed the plan had been downloaded straight from God.

After her creative writing students settled into their seats, Emily announced, "We're all going to share our basketball essays, but first, we're each going to write a second piece, and this time you're going to take the opposite viewpoint you took yesterday. So, if yesterday, you wrote 'Basketball is good for this island,' then today, you're going to write 'Basketball isn't good for this island.' Any questions?" She didn't give them a chance to raise any. "OK, good, get started."

There was some moaning and muttering, but they did all get started. Except for Hailey. She just sat there, her face worried.

"What is it, Hailey?" Emily whispered.

"I want to do this, Miss Morse, but I'm afraid I'll get in trouble."

*Shoot*, Emily thought. "OK, well, what if you type it up, and I'll read it right on your screen, and then we'll delete it? We never even have to print it out."

Hailey thought about that for a moment. "But I still will have written it. I still think Milton will find out."

Emily thought this completely ridiculous, but she saw real fear on Hailey's face and that made her heart hurt.

"OK." Emily lowered her voice even more. "Why don't you write a poem about something else right now? We'll just let you skip this part of the assignment."

Hailey's face lit up, which lit up Emily's heart. And just like that, she had done it again. Making special allowances for basketball players was becoming a habit.

# Chapter 16

James took her out to dinner that night. At the same restaurant. Where they both ordered beef. Again. She had offered to cook for him some night, but he had quoted Paul, "Give them no cause, lest the ministry be discredited."

After they'd ordered, she finally let go of the question that had been squirming to be set free. "How well do you know Milton Darling?"

James furrowed his handsome brow. "Why?"

"Because he's not very nice to me."

"What does that mean?"

"I mean, he's kind of a bully, so I thought maybe you could give me some insight as to how to deal with him." *And maybe even beat him up for me,* she added silently.

James shook his head. "I don't want to speak ill of him, but we weren't friends. He was an excellent player. Had two sisters who played too. His father was their coach. His father was a great coach, so Milton was a shoo-in for the job, and I have no evidence that he isn't a great coach too."

"What does that mean, you have no evidence?"

"Huh?"

"Why not just say, 'He's a great coach'? Saying you have no evidence makes it sound like you think he's *not* a great coach."

"I don't know, Emily." James sounded annoyed. "I don't really think much about basketball anymore. Is that what he's giving you trouble about, basketball?"

"Yes. I had the kids write an opinion piece about whether or not basketball is good for the island."

James paused, apparently letting his brain absorb this. Then, "What were you thinking?"

"What? The kids can't have opinions?"

"Well, no, not really. And if a player writes that basketball isn't good for this island, she's going to get benched, or worse."

"What do you mean worse?"

"I just mean the community might hold it against her."

"The community? Are you kidding? These are just kids! Doing an assignment! What is the big deal?"

James leaned forward. "I know you don't care about sports. I don't either, anymore, but most of this island *does* care, so can you just embrace it? Basketball is important here. It's what we have. It's what gets us through the winters."

*And we're back to the winter*, Emily thought. "So you're saying it's my fault that a grown man, a professional teacher, got in my face and hollered at me?"

"I didn't say that. He got in your face? I'll talk to him."

*Finally*.

"Is that OK? You mind if I talk to him? Don't want to embarrass you or anything."

"No. I would be grateful if you'd talk to him."


Emily asked Duke to share one of his basketball opinion pieces. He read a poignant piece about how basketball is just a stupid game that gives adults an excuse to act like children, and allows people who are miserable with their lives to live vicariously through their offspring.

Emily praised him for a well-organized essay and then asked him to read his second piece. He rolled his eyes, but he complied.

This one was a short poem, citing that basketball was good for exercise and for learning to be part of a team. He couldn't have sounded less sincere. As he sat back down, he said, "Hailey's turn."

Hailey shook her head.

"Would you like to share?" Emily asked her.

"No, thank you."

"OK, then, Thomas? Would you—"

"That's not fair!" Duke cried.

"Duke," Emily said, trying not to sound as exasperated as she felt, "no one made you read. You did, and you will get credit for your efforts. I'm not going to *make* anyone share anything personal that they wrote."

Duke crossed his arms and slumped in his chair. Everyone else shared their pieces, but no real revelations were made. The pro's all sounded pretty much the same, as though they'd been hearing them since birth, and the con's—with the exception of Duke's—all sounded like teen angst.

The bell rang, and people dropped their poems and essays on her desk. She shuffled through them till she found Hailey's, which were the only ones she hadn't heard.

## Basketball Is Good for This Island
By Hailey Leadbetter

# PIERCEHAVEN

My parents met at a basketball game. My mom is from Valley, and when her team came to play on the island, my dad's family hosted her. They say it was love at first sight. I'm not sure if this is true, but I do know that if it weren't for basketball, I wouldn't even exist.

I have been playing for as long as I can remember. I can't ever remember not loving basketball. I love it more than anything, other than my family, who also loves it.

I don't think I'd know who I was if it weren't for basketball. Basketball gives me something to do, something to care about, something to work hard for. I'm not sure what goals I would have or what I would spend my time on, if it weren't for ball.

As for the island, it's pretty much the same. What would everyone do all winter, if not cheer on the kids? Would they all sit around, drinking and watching television? I think so. Basketball gives us a sense of community. We all come together for it. We are all on the same side. When someone does fight about something, they can still come together in the gym and be friends.

If you take away basketball, this island only has one thing: lobsters. And while that's important, not everyone is a lobsterman. So what about the rest of us? What can we say we're good at? What can we take pride in? Nothing. That's why we need basketball.

A little short on word count, but not poorly written. On to part B of the assignment.

**Darkness**
By Hailey Leadbetter

The surface of the water looks so calm and peaceful
But just beneath it there is a sticky darkness
No one wants to touch or talk about
I am scared of this darkness
And I like to pretend it's not there
If no one talks about it
Will it go away
Is there anything I can do to make it
Go away
I work so hard, play so hard,
Think so hard, sweat so hard
So that maybe the darkness
Won't be real

# PIERCEHAVEN

Because I don't really know
Who the darkness is eating
Or who it will eat next
All I know is, it's not eating me
And maybe that's what makes me most sad
Why doesn't the darkness want me?

As she read the last line, she was already out of her chair and headed down the hall. "Have you seen Hailey?" she asked Hannah.

"She's probably already in the gym."

*Of course,* Emily thought, *basketball practice.*

She entered the gym, but it was empty. She trucked right through and into the locker room, where some girls were already changing.

"Miss Morse!" Jasmine gasped accusingly.

"Hailey, I need to talk to you!"

Hailey, not seeming too surprised, nodded, and slipped her practice jersey over her head. Then she headed out of the locker room and into the gym, where Milton was now rolling a bin of basketballs across the floor. He looked at them suspiciously.

"Not here," Emily muttered, and led Hailey out of the gym and down the hall to the conference room, which, blessedly, was empty.

Hailey entered the room and Emily closed the door.

"Look, it's nothing, just a poem. I wrote it in like two minutes."

"You said you weren't going to write about basketball."

"That's not about basketball."

"Then what's it about?"

"The ocean."

Emily looked down at the poem. "Hailey, I don't think this is about the ocean." She looked back at Hailey, who stood motionless and expressionless.

"Well, it is."

Emily sat down and pulled another chair out. "Sit, please."

"I can't be late for practice."

"I know that. And I won't make you late for practice. But please, talk to me, Hailey. Tell me what this poem's about."

Hailey plopped down in the chair. "It's not *about* anything, Miss Morse. I swear! It's just a poem."

Emily looked at the poem, and read the last line aloud, "'Why doesn't the darkness want me?' What does the darkness represent, Hailey?"

"Nothing. It's just the darkness under the water. You know, the part that doesn't get any sunlight."

Emily looked into Hailey's eyes, wishing she could see what was going on behind them. "Hailey, do you think about hurting yourself?"

Hailey laughed. "Oh! Is that what this is about? Miss Morse, I swear, I would *never* hurt myself. No way."

"OK, well, do you see how this poem might give me that idea?"

Hailey shrugged.

"Is the darkness death?"

"Miss Morse! I swear! It's not! It's just a poem! Can we just forget about it?"

Emily sighed. "Hailey, I am obligated by law, not to mention human decency, to tell the guidance counselor if I think you are in danger of hurting yourself."

Her eyes filled with tears. "Miss Morse, please. Don't. You will *ruin* my life if you do that."

"It wouldn't ruin your life. You would just get to talk to someone else about what you're going through—"

"I'm not going through anything! My life is perfect! I'm a basketball star! My parents don't abuse me! I've got straight A's! I promise, *nothing is wrong*!"

The conference door flew open. "What's going on?" Milton asked.

Emily instinctively flipped the poem over.

"What's that?"

"Nothing of your concern."

"Hailey, get to the gym."

Hailey slid through the door with speed and grace. Milton took two more steps into the room and then slammed the door. "What is your problem?"

Emily moved toward the door, but Milton blocked her path.

"Show me that piece of paper."

"No!" She tried to sound firm, but her voice, not to mention her whole body, was shaking. She made another move for the door.

He blocked her again and grabbed her arm with his left hand, while trying to wrestle the crumpled poem out of her right fist, which was squeezing as if she meant to hold on to life itself.

"Let go! You're hurting me!" She hated how screechy her voice sounded, how panicky, but there it was.

His grip on her arm tightened, and he actually managed to rip part of the paper from her hand. And then, as if it had a mind of its own, her right knee came up with sudden, incredible force and planted itself in his groin. He doubled over, and she ran out of the room, but she only made it across the hall, where she fled into the staff bathroom, locked the door, and then slid to the floor in a ball of tears. She smoothed out the poem and saw that yes, he had ripped the paper, but no, he hadn't gotten any of the actual poem.

"Thank you, Jesus," she breathed. And then she just sat there and cried for a while.

# Chapter 17

Emily lay awake most of the night, wondering why she had worked so hard to protect Hailey's poem from Milton's eyes. Then irrational fears began to stick their tentacles into her brain: Milton was in her driveway. Milton was at her window. Milton would be at her car in the morning, at the door of the school on Monday.

She began to pray. "Lord, I don't know what kind of hold this man has over me, but please set me free of it. I don't want to be terrified of the *phys ed* teacher." As she prayed, she felt her breathing slow, but then a new fear slinked in: the fear of getting in trouble. Sure, he had been rude, and he had grabbed her arm, but she had actually assaulted him. What if *he* went to the administration about *her*? Should she get out ahead of it? Go talk to Principal Hogan herself, and tell him everything? Or should she just pretend it never happened?

# PIERCEHAVEN

She prayed some more, and finally decided that she wouldn't decide. Instead, she would focus on dealing with the Hailey situation. One crisis at a time. She watched the Saturday sun come up through her bedroom window, and lay there for a while longer, waiting for the rest of the island to wake up.

When she thought she couldn't go another minute without coffee, she got out of bed and descended the spiral staircase in her bare feet, resisting the urge to look out the windows to make sure no one was looking in.

After a pot of coffee and a bagel, she drove to school. Her hand shook as she unlocked the door, and she couldn't help looking around the parking lot every three seconds. Finally, she was inside the dark, still foyer.

She went into the office and found the staff directory, which provided her the guidance counselor's home phone number.

"Can you come meet me at school? It's urgent."

The counselor, Richard Babcock, didn't sound happy about it, but he couldn't exactly refuse. Still, he took his time getting there, and she spent that time pacing around the dark main office, a bundle of nerves. She kept checking the main doors, scared that Milton would suddenly appear, so when they did open at Mr. Babcock's hand, she skittered back into a dark corner.

He entered the office and flicked on the lights, which felt uncomfortably bright to Emily.

"What is it?"

"Thank you so much for coming, Mr. Babcock. I really appreciate it—"

"What is it?" he repeated.

"I'm concerned that Hailey Leadbetter might be thinking about hurting herself."

He actually laughed. "Hailey? She's the healthiest kid we've got. Why would you say such a thing?"

"She wrote a poem that made me think she's in danger."

"OK, where's the poem?"

"I don't have it." This was a lie, but she thought it was a lesser sin than betraying Hailey's trust.

"You don't have it. So what did the poem say?"

"It talked about darkness, about how she was scared of the darkness, but how she also wanted it, or rather, she wanted it to want her."

"What? That doesn't even make sense."

"Can you just talk to her?"

"Of course. Is that all?"

She breathed out a long breath she hadn't realized she'd been holding. "Yes, that's all."

"What happened to your arm?"

She looked down at the purple bruises left by Milton's hand. "It's a long story."

"OK then. I'm going home. You have a good weekend."

"Can you talk to Hailey today?"

"I said I'd talk to her."

He never did.


On Sunday morning, Emily descended the stairs into the basement sanctuary, where James greeted her with a hug. She'd worn long sleeves, but when he squeezed both her arms, she winced. He pushed her sleeve up and his eyes grew wide. "What is this?"

"Milton."

"Are you serious?"

She nodded.

"What happened?"

"Can we talk about it later?"

"Let's talk about it now." He gently took her hand and led her back up the stairs and out of Abe's house. Safely on the brown lawn, he asked again, "What happened?"

She didn't know quite where to begin. "I was talking to one of his players, one of his *good* players, about a poem she had written, and he barged in, told her to get to practice, even though it hadn't even started yet, and then told me to give him the poem. I refused. So he grabbed my arm and tried to take the poem out of my hand. So I kicked him and ran away."

"You kicked him?"

"Well, *kneed* him."

"Where?"

"Where do you think?"

He took a step back, and she couldn't tell if he was horrified or amused. Maybe both. "All this over a poem?"

"No, all this because I dare to try to educate his basketball players, whom he apparently thinks he owns. I'm telling you, the man is shady!"

"I'll take care of it." He gave her a kiss on the cheek, sending a herd of butterflies through her gut, and then took long strides toward his pickup.

"What are you going to do?" she called after him.

"Don't worry about it," he called back.

*Easier said than done*, she thought. She headed back inside and down the stairs, praying the whole way.

# Chapter 18

James refused to tell Emily what had transpired between Milton and him, and that drove her nuts, but Milton also stopped hassling her after that weekend. In fact, he stopped everything. He didn't even look at her, and the language arts education of the Piercehaven high schoolers proceeded at a comfortable clip. No drama; no Milton. One could almost forget it was basketball season.

Until the day Emily found MacKenzie crying in the broom closet.

It was the second Monday in December, the Monday after their season openers. Both boys' and girls' teams had left school early on Friday—making the school feel much like a ghost town—to head northwest to Jackson. First, they all hopped on the ferry for the ninety-minute voyage. Then, the 150 mile trek to Jackson took them nearly four hours by bus, and they had to get there in time for the girls' game, which started at five.

After the games were over, and the gym finally emptied, the kids all rolled out their sleeping bags on the floor so that they could get some sleep, though most of them slept very little. Then they got up early and played two more basketball games—girls, then boys—before the long bus ride back to the ferry terminal.

So, when Emily found MacKenzie in the broom closet, she figured she must be fathoms beyond exhausted.

It happened during Emily's prep period, when MacKenzie was supposed to be in the library for study hall. Emily was on her way to the restroom when she heard sniffling in the closet. She stopped outside the door and leaned in to listen, but she didn't hear anything else. So she eased the door open and found MacKenzie sitting there in the dark, her arms around her legs, sobbing into her knees. She looked so incredibly young in that moment, and Emily went full-on maternal. She rushed in and scooched in front of her. "MacKenzie! What's wrong, honey?"

MacKenzie shook her head. "Nothing. Just leave me alone."

"Absolutely not." Emily stood. "Come on, we're going to my room."

MacKenzie didn't budge.

"Come on, honey. Don't worry. The hallway's empty."

MacKenzie did get up then, slowly, and with her arms folded across her chest and her chin as far down as it would go, she followed Emily back to her classroom.

Once they were seated behind a closed door, Emily said, "Spill it."

MacKenzie didn't look at her. She just shook her head. "It's nothing. I'm just having a bad day."

"Is it boy stuff?"

MacKenzie's head snapped up. "No!" She looked horrified.

Emily laughed. "OK, then. Good. So what is it?"

She looked down at her hands again. "Nothing."

Emily thought it might be better to just get her talking. "How did the games go?"

"Good."

"Can you tell me about them?"

"What do you want to know?"

"Well, did you have fun?"

MacKenzie looked up at her and snorted. "Basketball isn't fun."

"Oh?" This surprised Emily. Not so much that basketball wasn't fun, but that MacKenzie would admit it so readily. "Then why do you play?"

"I have to. We all have to. It's just what we do." She paused. Then added with some reluctance, "And it is fun. Sometimes. But playing at Jackson isn't much fun. We killed them."

"I heard that. And the boys won too?"

"Jackson isn't very good this year."

"I see. So how did you play?"

"Good I guess."

Emily resisted the urge to correct her grammar. "What position do you play?"

"I'm a one."

"I don't know what that means."

"I'm the point guard. I run the offense."

"Wow, that sounds like a lot of pressure for a sophomore in high school."

"I've been doing it a long time," she said, and Emily heard some pride in her voice.

"How do you get along with your teammates?"

"Good. We fight, but like sisters, not really enemies. Some of us *are* sisters." She giggled a little. And she wasn't crying anymore.

"You don't have a sister on the team, do you?"

"No, but Chloe is my cousin."

"And how do you get along with her?"

"OK," she said, but it didn't ring true.

Emily wanted to keep her talking, but she was running out of questions. She didn't really have any intelligent questions to ask about basketball. "MacKenzie, I just want you to know that I really care about you."

MacKenzie looked at her suspiciously.

"I mean, it's not just about English. I care about whether you can read and write, but I also care about you as a whole person. And if something's wrong, I want to help—"

"I'm OK," MacKenzie said, sitting up straighter in the chair. "I should probably be getting back to study hall." She stood to go.

"OK, well, just know that my door is always open."

MacKenzie walked to the door, opened it, and then turned to look at Emily. "Thanks, Miss M. But I'm OK, really."

# Chapter 19

Emily asked Chloe to stay after creative writing. Once everyone else had left, she said, "So I've been talking to you pretty openly about God and church and stuff, and I want you to tell me if I ever make you uncomfortable with any of that, OK?"

Chloe scrunched her eyebrows together. "I'll never be uncomfortable with Jesus, Miss Morse."

Emily laughed. "That's good to hear. But I just—it's hard for me to walk this line between public educator and follower of Jesus. I'm just sort of figuring it out as I go." She paused. "So, I want to ask you something, and you totally don't have to do it."

"OK," she said, dragging out the K as if she wasn't sure whether she was OK with anything.

"I want you to invite MacKenzie to church."

"MacKenzie Ginn? To *our* church? As in Noah's basement?"

Emily laughed again. "Yeah. If you're comfortable with it."

"Why can't you do it?"

"I could. But I'm really not supposed to, and I think it would carry more weight coming from you." Emily knew that the former reason was the stronger motivator for her, but she tried to emphasize the latter with her voice.

Chloe took a deep breath. "Can I think about it?"

"Of course."

"She's going to make fun of me."

"You don't have to do it."

"Her dad's not a super nice man. He doesn't believe."

"OK. Like I said, it was just a thought. You don't have to. So, how was Jackson?"

Chloe groaned. "It's a *long* bus ride."

"I can imagine."

"*Super* curvy roads. I was carsick half the trip."

"I'm sorry to hear that. How did you play?"

"Good. I scored three three-pointers in the first game and five in the second."

"Wow!"

"Yeah. It was pretty great."

"What position do you play?"

"I'm a two."

"I don't know what that means."

"It means I'm a shooting guard."

"Oh, well that makes sense."

"Yep. Gotta go. We've got early practice today. But I'll ask her, Miss Morse."

"OK great. I think it'll be good."


MacKenzie was at Bible study two nights later. She came with Chloe and her parents. They came hurrying down the stairs just before the six o'clock start time.

Emily didn't always go to the Wednesday night meetings, but she was glad she did this time. She tried to give MacKenzie a big welcoming smile, but MacKenzie went to great pains to avoid eye contact.

MacKenzie wasn't the only new face either. There were two other people Emily didn't recognize.

There was a scripture reading, and then a short discussion about what they'd just read. Then a woman named Darcy stood up to give her testimony. She looked incredibly nervous, but she cleared her throat and spoke clearly and loudly, "My name is Darcy, and I just felt like God really wanted me to share my story tonight. I don't have a really exciting story like some people. I've never been to prison or been addicted to drugs." She laughed awkwardly. "But I used to be really lost. I used to be really confused. I didn't know what was true about life. I didn't know what to believe, or who to believe. I had all these people telling me all these different things, and they all claimed that they loved me, but I never really *felt* loved by any of them." She took a deep breath. "I'm not sure if any of this is making any sense."

"It is, it is," people encouraged from the small audience.

Darcy smiled and continued, "So then one day, a friend of mine"—she pointed to a woman in the second row—"told me about the gospel. And I'd heard about Jesus a little bit throughout my life, but I had never really heard the story about *why* he'd come to earth and *why* he'd died. And then she told me ..." The tears started then, and her voice began to crack, so she slowed the words down. "She told me that Jesus loves me. And that he's the only one I need to be listening to, that he's the only one who is real, that all these other voices"—she waved her hands around her head as if battling black flies—"are just ... noise. And so I listened to that friend, and I prayed to Jesus that day. I asked him to come into my life. I asked him to show himself to me. I said, 'If you died for me, then I guess I can believe in you.' And he did. He showed up, and I felt my whole body fill with this love, this real love, this love that felt like nothing else in my whole life had ever felt. For the first time, I felt like everything just sort of made sense, like I didn't know how it would happen, but that everything would be OK. And even if it wasn't OK, it *was* OK, because I was loved." She took a deep breath. "Now, would you all do something for me? I've never actually led anyone in a salvation prayer, but I'm thinking now's the time to start. I know most of you know Jesus, but just in case one of you doesn't, would you please pray with me? Would you please bow your heads and close your eyes? I just want to say a simple prayer, and if you've never prayed to Jesus before, I beg you to pray this prayer with me. You don't have to do it out loud. Just say it in your head, and I promise … I promise, it will *change* your life. OK, here goes … Jesus, thank you for coming to earth as a man. Thank you for dying on the cross. Thank you for loving me. Please forgive me for all the times I've messed up. Please come into my life. Please, show me that you are real. Please let me feel that love that the Bible talks so much about. Please come into my life and change it. Thank you, Jesus. Amen." There was a small pause, and Emily wondered if she could raise her head yet, but Darcy continued, "If you just prayed that prayer with me, would you please raise your hand just a little? I won't embarrass you. I won't point you out. I just want to know, so that I can pray for you, and so that I can come talk to you later. Oh, bless your heart, sweetie, thank you for raising your hand. The angels are singing in heaven right now because of you. Is there anyone else? … Anyone? OK, I thank you all for listening to me. Have a great night." She grabbed a few more tissues and returned to her seat. Emily stole a glance at MacKenzie, whose face was shiny with tears, and whose head was on her aunt's shoulder.

Emily wanted to pry, to snoop, to lurk around the basement and find out what had happened with MacKenzie, but she was surrounded by family, including Chloe, and Emily figured she was in good hands. Instead, she prayed during the short drive home, she prayed as she entered her home, as she brushed her teeth, as she ascended her stairs, as she slipped into bed, and as she drifted off to sleep. She prayed for MacKenzie.

On Thursday morning, Emily found Chloe alone in her classroom. Emily looked pointedly into her eyes, and said, "Thank you."

Chloe, apparently knowing exactly what she meant, said, "You were right. You were so right. MacKenzie is really amped up about Jesus right now. She was at our house until almost midnight, talking to my parents about God."

"Wow!" Emily took off her jacket and sat down. "What do MacKenzie's parents think?"

"Not sure yet."

"Darcy's testimony was pretty incredible, wasn't it?"

"Yes! Especially since she like, never talks. Seriously, she's wicked quiet. I've never heard her say much of anything."

"God must have really wanted her to speak up then. And I'd say it's a good thing she did." Emily looked around her room. "Where's Thomas?"

"He's home sick. At least, he says he's sick. Sometimes he takes what he calls 'mental health days.'"

"Ah, yes, well, sometimes those are necessary, though Thomas has always struck me as someone with optimum mental health."

"Maybe that's because he takes mental health days."

"Excellent point. So I've been meaning to ask you, are you two … an item?"

Chloe laughed. "An item? No one says that, Miss Morse. But no, we are not *an item*. Not even close. Thomas is just … well, he's just Thomas."

"Well, *just Thomas* would have to be crazy not to be crazy about you."

# Chapter 20

On Monday morning, the school was abuzz with excitement. Both teams had just returned with double victories over Gould. But most people were talking about the fact that Hailey had scored 34 points on Saturday morning, which was a new school record.

As Julie, the office administrator, read the game stats over the intercom, Emily handed back papers, so she had the perfect vantage point to catch Sydney rolling her eyes at the announcement and congratulations of Hailey's accomplishment.

"Is that some jealousy I see?" Emily said softly, so no one else could hear.

"No, my back just hurts from sleeping on the stupid gym floor."

"I'm sorry your back hurts, but eye rolls are not a typical response to physical pain."

Sydney rolled her eyes again. "I'm not jealous. But now all anyone is going to talk about is her getting her thousand points her junior year. It's just annoying."

Emily gave up and moved on, handing a paper back to Victoria, who was sitting there motionless and emotionless, staring at the floor in front of her.

"Are you OK, Vic?" Emily asked.

She looked up, seemingly surprised to find Emily standing there, and then nodded. "Yeah. Just tired, I guess."

"I bet you are. I don't know how you guys keep up this pace. I'm exhausted just hearing about it."

The day flew by, and soon it was lunch.

Kyle popped his head into her room seconds after the bell. "Mind if I eat in here?"

"Come on in. I've already eaten, though. Just grading papers now."

"Ah, just give 'em all B's." He laughed at his own joke as he pulled up a chair and took some leftover Chinese food out of a paper bag. "Don't blame you, though. If I had fifth period prep, I'd have already eaten too."

"Chinese food? Smells like someone's been off the island."

"Oh, absolutely. Every chance I get."

"Well it beats a protein bar, I suppose."

"That it does. Egg roll?" He held out his offering.

"No thanks."

"Suit yourself. So, how are things going?"

"Good. Great, actually. Though I'm thinking of going to the mainland myself soon."

"Good for you!" He shoved an entire chicken finger into his mouth.

"Tomorrow night, the kids play Camden Christian. I thought I'd go check it out."

"They'll have home games, you know," he said through a full mouth.

"I know, but won't it mean more if I go to an away game? And it's the closest away game, by a long stretch."

He nodded, twirling his chopsticks busily. "That it is. That's a long ferry ride for a basketball game, though. And you'd have to spend the night."

"I know. Still, seems like it might be a fun adventure."

"Your kittens aren't going to like it."

"They're cats. They'll be fine."

"You want some company?"

She looked at him. "You just said it was a bad idea."

He shrugged and smiled mischievously. "You're talking me into it."

"Well, you're welcome to come, of course, but you should know, I'm also going to ask James to come along."

"Oh, of course you are."

There was a knock on the open door. Emily looked up to see MacKenzie standing awkwardly in the doorway. "What's up, MacKenzie?"

"Can I talk to you for a sec?"

"Of course!" Emily started to get up, but Kyle interrupted.

"No, no, stay. I'll get out of your way." He got up and left the room, smiling at MacKenzie on his way out. But he only took one container of food with him, so Emily figured he'd be back soon.

"What's up?" Emily asked again.

"Um ... well ... I just wanted you to know, because I figured you would've heard by now, about what Milton told Hailey to tell me ..."

Emily flinched, still not used to the players calling their coach (not to mention their phys ed teacher and athletic director) by his first name. "What did he tell Hailey to tell you?"

MacKenzie looked at the ceiling and blew her blonde bangs out of her face, a mannerism that made her look so young. "Well, he told Hailey to tell me that he didn't want me talking to you anymore. Like, I can still talk to you about English, but that's it. No other stuff. See, my teammates have been asking me questions about all this Jesus stuff, and I've been answering them, so well, so now Milton blames you. Sorry. He thinks .... he says, you're a bad influence on me."

"OK," Emily said slowly. "I hadn't heard any of that yet."

"Well, you would've eventually, there are no secrets on an island, not really, so I just wanted to be the one to tell you, so that I could also tell you that I'm going to ignore it. You know, I think it's kind of stupid."

Emily waited for her to say more. When she didn't, Emily said, "All right then. Thanks for telling me. I appreciate your wisdom."

MacKenzie gave her a wide grin, turned and bounced out of the room, her burden obviously lifted. Kyle reappeared instantaneously.

"Did you catch all that, snoop?"

"Oh yeah. There's no secrets on an island." He smirked and slid back into his chair. "Don't let it bother you."

"I won't."

He looked skeptical.

"No really, I won't. I'm done letting Milton bother me."

That night, Emily called James from her landline. She didn't do this often, as he wasn't much of a phone conversationalist. He didn't seem to mind long, empty pauses, gaps in the conversation that drove her nuts, and then she would rush to fill them and end up saying something embarrassing, something she would agonize over for hours to follow. It was simpler to just avoid the phone. But she really needed to talk to him this time. She wanted him to go to Camden with her.

"Hullo?"

"Hey, it's me. I was wondering if you wanted to go watch the teams play against Camden Christian tomorrow?"

"They're playing away."

"Yeah, I know that."

"So, they'll have home games, you know."

"Yeah, people keep telling me that. I still want to go."

"I don't think that's such a good idea."

"Why not?"

"Because it's December. On a ferry. It's not a short trip, you know."

"Yeah. I've made the trip, James."

"Well, if you want to go, go. But I don't want to spend three hours on a ferry, in the winter, to go watch us slaughter a Christian school."

"What does that have to do with anything?"

"I meant that Christian schools are even smaller than we are, and so their teams aren't very good. The score is going to be a hundred to two. Besides, where are you going to spend the night?"

"I thought I'd get a hotel."

There was that awkward pause.

"I'm not asking *you* to get a hotel room with me, James. You know what, I'm sorry I asked. I'm going to go. I'll talk to you when I get home." *Maybe*, she thought, as she hung up the phone.

# Chapter 21

Hailey waited until the other three students in AP English had left the room and then approached Emily's desk. "You wanna tell me how I got a B on this?"

Emily looked up, surprised. "First of all, I don't like your tone. Second, have you looked at the rubric?"

"Yes!"

"All right, and did you understand the rubric?"

"Of course."

"Well then you should be able to see how you didn't quite meet the standard for grammar with this assignment."

"Miss Morse, I *can't* get a B! I'm only 0.2 points ahead of Hannah right now, and I *have* to be valedictorian! You are messing with my future right now!"

"Hailey, I am sorry you are upset, but why don't we talk about this when you can be calmer and more respectful. I've got another class coming in."

Actually, they were already in.

Hailey leaned toward her and lowered her voice. "Is this about MacKenzie?"

"Oh for heaven's sake, Hailey. Of course not. This is about you having ten comma splices in that essay. I am an adult, and a professional. I know you are not necessarily used to dealing with adults like me, but I don't play petty games. Now go to your next class." Emily pointed at the door, and Hailey looked as though she'd been slapped. She looked around the room, appearing to only just then notice all the seniors staring at her, and then, flushed, she grabbed her bag and hurried out of the room.

Emily speed-walked down the ferry plank. James had been right about one thing. It *was* cold. She hurried onto the boat and into the warm cabin, where rows of hard, plastic seats faced dirty windows. Most of the seats were already full of players and parents. She avoided Milton's glare and decided to try the starboard cabin instead.

This cabin was nearly as full, but with the boys' team. She found a seat and leaned her head against a bulkhead, clutching her oversized purse (which contained clothes and toothbrush) in her lap, and closed her eyes.

Somehow, she managed to fall asleep like this, despite the constant chatter of teenage boys and the low rumble of bow thrusters, and didn't wake up till they were docking in Camden. *Wow,* she thought, *I'm turning into a regular islander.* She yawned and stretched, but stayed in her seat as the boys were clogging the doorway.

Finally, the boat docked and plank secured, the boys burst through the doorway, and she followed. She marveled at the energy of the young athletes as they all trotted up the plank, and she slowly climbed up after them.

An idling bus sat in the parking lot, and she watched the last of her students climb aboard. Sydney caught her eye and shouted, "You want a ride, Miss Morse?" but before Emily could answer, Milton reached around Sydney and shut the bus door.

Trying not to be offended, Emily trudged through the salty slush and into the ferry terminal to call a cab.

When she got to the gym, she understood a little better why James hadn't wanted to come. The gym, which appeared to double as a sanctuary, was tiny, and there was only one set of bleachers. Emily wasn't even sure she'd be able to find a seat, but she finally managed to squeeze in on the very front row.

After a short wait, the mighty Lady Panthers burst out onto the floor, and the crowd went wild. Emily looked around and concluded that there were more Panther fans present than Camden Christian Conqueror fans.

The appearance of her girls (she'd come to think of them that way) startled her. They looked so *different*. First of all, their outfits must have cost a fortune. They had shiny warm-ups over their uniforms, the kind that button up the leg so they can be ripped off in one fell swoop. Each of them had her last name emblazoned across her back. They looked like the Celtics, only red and white. And they all had matching shoes. Red and white Nikes. Emily felt a twinge of indignation over her salary, but then remembered that she was living rent-free, and the twinge went away.

The Conquerors ran out onto the court, and the crowd cheered again, though with noticeably less oomph than their first go-round. These kids wore mismatched shorts and T-shirts with numbers stuck on the back. One girl's number appeared to be crafted out of blue duct tape.

# PIERCEHAVEN

Some of the Panthers were already ripping their pants off, and Emily was dismayed to see that even their socks matched. Who was paying for all this stuff?

Eventually, the shock brought on by their apparel faded, and she was able to admire the elegance of their warmup routine. They went through their lines, first layups, then jump shots, gracefully, each player using the same form as the last, as if they were all clones. But it was somehow mesmerizing, and Emily found it really neat to see her girls in such a new and different way.

After someone announced the girls' names and a pale young Conqueror sang the national anthem with fear and trembling, the girls took the floor for the jump ball. Jasmine didn't even have to jump, but she did anyway, and expertly flicked the ball to MacKenzie, who dribbled it all the way in for a layup, as if there wasn't even another team on the floor.

A defeated-looking Conqueror inbounded the ball to their team's version of MacKenzie, but the Panthers' MacKenzie was all over her, and soon had stripped her of the ball and scored again. Emily would be the first to admit she didn't know much about sports, but she was starting to feel like a bully. The crowd behind her had no such notion, though, and continued to scream with what sounded like bloodlust.

Finally, the Conquerors got the ball across half-court, and even got a shot off, but Jasmine scooped up the rebound, then turned and fired the ball the length of the court, without even looking, to MacKenzie, who just happened to be there waiting. *It is like they're telepathic*, Emily thought, remembering what Chloe had told her.

At one point, MacKenzie brought the ball up the court slowly, looking at the whole floor before her, and Emily could almost see the gears moving in her brain. She'd never seen her so focused, so serious. And she had a presence about her, one that her team seemed to recognize. There was no doubt about it—Hailey might be the star, but this sophomore spitfire was *in charge*.

A few steps past half court, MacKenzie quadrupled her speed, dribbled right into the paint, and as the defense collapsed in on her, she flicked it back out to Chloe, who sank her first three-pointer of the night.

Emily was also surprised by the court-presence of senior Lexi Smith, the starting power forward, or as the girls would say, the "four." Lexi was quiet, nearly silent, in school, but out on the court, she was assertive and confident. Emily felt she was watching an entirely different kid.

Finally, Camden Christian managed to score. MacKenzie had lost track of the girl she was guarding, and the girl had ended up open under the basket. MacKenzie tried to recover, but was far too late, and reached the girl just in time to foul her as she let go of the ball.

Milton came flying off his seat. "Are you freakin' kidding me?" he screamed. His hands flew up to his sparse hair as if he was about to rip it out. "Are you kidding me, Ginn?" His face was purple, and veins were poking out of his neck.

Emily was horrified on MacKenzie's behalf, and deeply, deeply embarrassed. But when she looked around the gym, no one else seemed to think this outburst was even worth noticing. Even MacKenzie didn't really react. She just looked at Milton and nodded, then bent over and rested on her knees while the girls lined up for a foul shot.

But he wasn't done. "You know better than that!" he screamed. "You knew that screen was coming! You've got to get around it! Don't be lazy!"

Emily was astounded at MacKenzie's composure. If someone had hollered at her like that when she was fifteen, she would have been a puddle of tears on the hardwood. She snuck another look at Milton. She just couldn't understand why he was so upset. The score was 12 to 2.

At the end of the first quarter, the score had crept up to 16 to 4, and Milton finally took his starters out.

Sydney, Victoria, Ava, Natalie, and Hannah took the floor, but they were still far more skilled than the Conquerors, and the half ended with the score at 26 to 8.

At half-time, Emily decided to find a restroom, and, quite by accident, passed the room where the Panthers were having their break. A loud crash startled her, but the crash was followed by Milton's voice, which ironically, calmed her down. *Oh, is that all? He's just shouting again?* She did, however, wonder who his victim was this time.

When the girls returned to the court, Emily scanned their faces, but they all looked unscathed. Nary a tear in sight. *They must be used to it*, she thought. *Just par for the course.* Then she corrected herself for mixing sports.

During the second half, Emily started to figure some things out. This really was a beautiful thing. These girls were good at something, really good, and they were good at it together. It was like synergy, and she could see then why it mattered. Maybe not why it mattered quite as much as it did, but still. Her heart was warmed watching Natalie Greem, senior, and sister Kylie Greem, seventh grader, play on the floor together. Where else could that happen? She felt some pride about being from Piercehaven, about being part of the Piercehaven tradition, even if she was very much on the periphery of it.

After the game, Emily took out her cell, which actually worked for once, since she wasn't in the middle of the ocean, and started to call for a cab, but a woman stopped her. "Hi, I'm Heather, MacKenzie's mom. Do you have a place to stay?"

"Yes, the Camden Inn?"

"Us too. I don't think much else is open this time of year. Would you like a ride?"

"That would be great. Thanks." Emily picked up her bag and followed MacKenzie's mom out of the gym.

"The kids'll sleep in here tonight," Heather explained, "but I stopped sleeping on gym floors the day of my last basketball game. I don't care how much a motel costs."

# Chapter 22

There were only three days until Christmas vacation, and Emily still didn't know what she was going to do when that final bell rang. She'd been waiting for James to give her some idea as to what he wanted or expected her to do. But he'd been acting as though Christmas was still months away.

Emily's mother, of course, wanted her to come home for a week. Emily was fine with that idea, but was she supposed to invite James? She was terrified to ask, worried he might just say, "Why would I go home to meet your parents? We're just friends, you know." The truth was, she *didn't* know. She had no idea. She and James were two people who went out once a week and occasionally shared a kiss on the cheek. Of course she had feelings for him beyond that, but she didn't know for sure if he reciprocated those feelings.

She assumed he did, because he kept asking her out for meals. But maybe the man just really liked going to restaurants, and needed an excuse.

She didn't know. But she also liked him enough to keep going along with the pattern. An almost-relationship with him was better than a relationship with someone else. She really liked him. She liked the way he made her feel when she was around him—safe, giddy, and hopeful. But he also infuriated her with the way he seemed content with the way things were.

So, Emily refused to answer her mother, as James refused to answer the question Emily refused to ask. It was the world's strangest standoff.

On Friday morning, she gave up and emailed her mother that yes, she would be home that evening. Then she called James's answering machine: "Hey, I'm catching the last ferry today. Was wondering if we could meet up before we go. I have something for you." She had bought him a hand-sewn pillow, with a picture of a fishing vessel and Mark 4:39 embroidered on it.

When she went to the restroom during lunch, Julie flagged her down with his reply: "I'll meet you in the ferry line." She wasn't even sure why, but this response annoyed her.

It didn't take her long to pack. She threw all her clothes into a suitcase, and then packed her kittens into carriers she had borrowed from the vet. She hadn't told her mom they were coming, but she could hardly justify heating her house while she was gone, just for two cats. And she certainly wasn't going to leave them there with no heat.

She made it to the ferry line the requisite thirty minutes early. She still didn't understand why she had to be there so early, but people loved to tell tales of missing their ferry because they were only twenty-eight minutes early.

She was on the verge of tears while waiting in her car. She didn't want to leave the island. She didn't want to leave James. She was mad at herself for being so emotionally invested in such an emotionally distant man.

The terminal signs read "No unnecessary idling of engines," but she thought, with it being fifteen degrees out, the idling was necessary.

She didn't even see James coming, so he startled her when he opened the passenger side door and slid in. "You're going home?"

"Yep," she said, even though if he had asked her to change her plans, she would've.

He looked out the windshield, his jaw clenched.

"Everything OK?" she asked.

"Yep," he said, without looking at her. "I just didn't know you were going home." He handed her a small, wrapped package, still without looking at her.

"Thanks," she said, her voice practically vibrating with uncertainty. "Hang on." She turned to reach into the back and started madly unzipping things, looking for his gift, which she finally found. She turned back toward the front and held it out to him. Then she looked down at her own gift. "Do you want me to unwrap it now?"

"If you want."

"Well, do you want me to?"

He looked at her then. "Just do what you want, Emily. You always do."

"What on earth is that supposed to mean?"

"It means I had no idea you were leaving the island! And I still don't know how long you'll be gone, but I'm assuming you won't be back in time for Christmas, as you just handed me this box."

It was her turn to stare out the windshield, as she tried to hide the tears now spilling out of her eyes. "James, I waited and waited for you to say something, but when you didn't, I figured you didn't care what I did this week."

"I'm sorry, Emily. I thought I still had time. I've been pretty busy, you know."

She didn't know. "Doing what? You laid up the boat weeks ago." She still wasn't looking at him, but she could feel his eyes on her.

After several painfully silent seconds, he said, "Merry Christmas," and got out of the car.

And still crying, she drove onto the ferry.

And not till after she shut her car off, did she open his gift. Nestled inside a gift box, among fluffy tissue paper, was a silver bracelet. On one side, the engraving read, "SOS 4:9." At first she thought he was calling for help. But then she flipped it over, where the engraving read, "You have captured my heart."

She stopped breathing. Then she turned around to see the growing distance between the stern and the dock. It was far too late to get off the ferry. And she wouldn't be able to call him for at least an hour and a half. She clutched her new bracelet to her chest and cried.

One hundred long minutes later, she drove off the ferry, practically pushing the car in front of her up the ramp. Then she parked in the first spot she found and called James.

She was surprised that he answered. "I am so, so sorry, James."

"It's OK. I'm sorry too. I just figured you were staying on the island. I didn't think to ask."

"I can come back tomorrow morning? I'll take the first ferry back."

"No, it's OK. Spend some time with your folks. I'll be here when you get back."

# Chapter 23

Emily returned to the island on New Year's Day with both nervous excitement and a sense of foreboding. She felt she'd been gone for a long time, and was worried things had changed. What if people didn't like her anymore?

She'd missed her island home, but she'd also enjoyed her break away, where there were more people and everything just felt more *normal*. She'd liked having a cell phone again. And her old library. And her old church.

Her cats hadn't liked Plainfield, though, and had spent most of the week hiding behind the couch.

On Monday morning, Emily was excited to see her students. She drove into the parking lot with a giddy feeling in her stomach and a new bracelet on her wrist.

Even though she was earlier than usual, Thomas and Chloe were already in her classroom. "Do you guys sleep in here?" she joked.

They were excited to tell her about their Christmas, and their New Year's. Apparently, they'd received lots of presents, especially Thomas, who'd gotten a new game console that cost a fortune. And apparently, there had been a giant New Year's Eve party at a senior's house, and many a bad decision had been made. Chloe hadn't attended, but Thomas had, and he was eager to tattle on everyone he'd seen there. Emily heard a few basketball players' names and raised an eyebrow. "Aren't they under contract?"

"Pfft! Yeah, but those contracts don't mean anything. Half the girls drink with the coach!"

"Thomas!" Chloe snapped, and Thomas snapped his mouth shut, looking chagrined.

"Thomas?" Emily said slowly, looking from one face to another. "Is that true?"

Chloe was glaring at him.

"I dunno. Probably just rumors," Thomas said.

Emily looked at Chloe. "Chloe, is it true?"

"No."

"Because if it is, you wouldn't lie to protect him, would you?"

Chloe looked at her. "It's not true, Miss M. I know he can be a jerk sometimes, but Milton is a good coach."

"OK, then," Emily said, opening her laptop. She wanted to believe it wasn't true, but the way Thomas had first said it had sure made it sound like well-known fact.

The bell rang and Chloe and Thomas sauntered off as her freshmen filed in. She was surprised by how happy she was to see them, and greeted each of them by name.

That morning's announcement included an invitation for volunteers to host basketball players in their homes the coming weekend.

"Are you going to host?" Tyler asked Emily.

"I don't think so."

Oh, but she *was* going to host. Julie tracked her down during her prep period. "I don't have you on the host list yet."

"OK," Emily said.

"Has Lauren or Mike talked to you yet?"

"Uh … no. Why, do they want me to host?"

"I would assume so."

"OK, then, I'll host," she said, because she wasn't sure what else to say.

"OK, great," Julie said and turned to walk away.

"Wait! Can you tell me a little about how this works?"

# PIERCEHAVEN

Julie turned around and looked at her as if she were stupid. "You pick them up at the gym Friday evening and take them to your house. You'll get girls. Two of them. Sometimes you'll get a coach too, but you probably won't, as you don't really have room."

Julie's apparent knowledge of the capacity of Emily's home unnerved her.

"OK, but I'm not sure I even have room for two girls. All I have is a couch. Unless one of them wants to sleep on the floor."

"Your couch is a pullout," Julie said matter-of-factly.

*So creepy*, Emily thought.

"You take them home and feed them. Then wake them up on Saturday morning, feed them again, let them shower, and then bring them to the gym. That's it," she said, as if that was no small charge.

"And parents are all OK with this? I would think in this day and age, they might not want their kids sleeping in strange houses. I mean, they don't know me from Adam."

"This is Piercehaven," Julie said. "Things like that don't happen here."

This didn't really answer Emily's question, but she didn't really want to be further patronized by the school secretary, so she smiled and said, "OK, thanks."

# Chapter 24

On Friday night, the girls beat Seacoast Christian by 28 points. Emily assumed that she could take her guests home after the game, and she stood by the door waiting for someone to tell her which girls were her charge. But no one did. She watched the Seacoast Christian girls come out of the locker room and climb into the bleachers to watch the boys' game, and she realized with a sinking feeling that she too was expected to wait until after the boys' game. This was no big deal, really. She was happy to watch the boys play. It was the idea of being *expected* to also stay for the boys' game that annoyed her. Mandatory attendance of basketball games and mandatory hosting of children from other schools had not been mentioned in her job interview. Although, she realized, it might be in the fine print of her free rental agreement. So, with a resigned sigh, she too sat down to watch the boys' game.

# PIERCEHAVEN

The Piercehaven boys also crushed their opponent, though not quite as handily as the girls had done.

Not long after the final whistle, the announcer asked all girls' hosts to come to center court. Emily headed toward the circle painted in the center of their cafeteria, and recognized most of the other hosts as parents of female players. *Oh that must be fun*, she thought, *get clobbered by an opposing team and then get to sleep in their house*.

She was assigned two petite, quiet, incredibly polite girls named Ashley and Jodi.

They awkwardly followed her out to her cold car and climbed in wordlessly.

The silence of the dark car made it seem even colder. "Sorry, by the time the car warms up, we'll be to my house." She laughed nervously.

They said nothing.

"So, have you guys stayed over on Piercehaven before?"

"No," Ashley said.

"Yes, ma'am," Jodi said.

"Where did you stay, Jodi?"

"I don't remember. It was two years ago. I stayed with a teacher."

"Ah, I see." She pulled into her driveway. "Well, this is it. My humble abode."

"I think this is the same place I stayed last time."

Emily gave them some food choices. They chose cereal. "Don't you want to save that for breakfast?" she asked.

Jodi looked at her. "You don't have enough for both?"

"Oh, I do. I just didn't know if you wanted cereal for both meals."

Jodi looked at Ashley, then back at Emily. "We do."

"Wow, you guys are easy. OK, then, help yourselves."

She watched them eat, then gave them the nickel tour of the place. "Make yourselves at home, and let me know if you need anything. Your game tomorrow is at ten, correct? So what time do you want me to wake you up?"

"We're supposed to be there at 9:15. So, maybe 8:15?" Jodi said.

"Deal," Emily said. "I'll see you then. Good night." And she headed up her spiral staircase.

As she went, she heard Ashley say, "She doesn't even have a TV."

# Chapter 25

The following weekend, Piercehaven was to play at Vinalhaven. Emily realized fairly early in the week that there was some rivalry between these two island schools.

"Will you guys get host families or will you have to sleep in the gym?" Emily asked Victoria on Monday morning.

"We get families."

"Ah, so hosting is more of an island thing than a Piercehaven thing?"

Victoria gave her a dirty look. "It was a Piercehaven thing first. They copied us."

"How could you possibly know that?" Emily asked.

Victoria looked confused.

"I think she's right," Tyler piped up. "At least that's what people always say."

"I see. Do you ever wonder what they say on Vinalhaven?"

"They say, 'Come one, come all, tourists, we love you!" Tyler said, trying to sound seductive, and the whole class laughed.

After the laughter died down, Emily asked, "Do you ever wonder why tourism is bigger on Vinalhaven than here?"

"No," Tyler said. And the matter was closed.

Despite the fact that Vinalhaven was less than ten miles away by boat, the teams had to take the ferry back to Camden, then take a bus to Rockland, and a ferry out to Vinalhaven. And the students complained about this impending journey all week long.

"Why can't you just have a lobster boat shuttle you guys out there?" Emily asked Chloe one morning.

Chloe shrugged. "Dunno. This is just the way it's always been done. It sucks."

"Well, maybe it's not worth it to play Vinalhaven. Isn't there an easier school to play?"

Chloe shook her head. "We *have* to play them. We have to beat them. Every year. It's almost as important as the state game. Besides, we only have to do it every other year. On the other years, they have to come to us. So it's kind of worth it, knowing they will get their turn."

Thomas shook his head. "There's something wrong with you, Chloe."

Despite all the hubbub, Emily did manage to get some work out of the students that week, before they left Friday morning at ten. Kyle and Emily watched the backs of the red jerseys file down the hallway, a whole collection of white numbers walking away from them. "It's like, why even bother having school on Fridays?" she said.

"Wait till baseball," he said. "They leave even earlier, because the games start earlier in the day."

"Baseball? What about softball?"

"We don't have a softball team."

"Why not?"

Kyle shrugged. "Not enough interest I guess. On Piercehaven, it's basketball or nothing."

"But don't the girls complain? That the boys get something they don't?"

"Occasionally we'll get a girl on the baseball team. That's about it." He turned to go back into his room, which now held only one student.

Emily turned to go back to hers, which held zero. She didn't know the first thing about sports, but somehow, this new knowledge of how the Piercehaven spring season worked niggled at her. What if a girl wanted to play a sport just for fun, or just for exercise? Was crazy-intense-life-or-death basketball really her only choice? Or what if a basketball player wanted to do something else, just for a change of pace? They probably weren't allowed, she thought. Because they play basketball year round. She'd already heard that girls were told they couldn't go skiing, as it might hurt their knees, or snowmobiling, as it was bad for the back.

Both teams returned to Piercehaven still undefeated, but there was worry that their number one ranking might not last. Emily hadn't known, but Piercehaven's season schedule had come out a little lopsided, with all of the "hard" games on the backside.

"Is that really a big deal?" she asked Chloe. "Now you'll go into the tough games confident, right?"

"Or cocky. Valley's good. They come here this weekend, but we should be able to beat them. But then we have to go to Rangeley, and they're undefeated too. That's who we played in the Southern Maine finals last year. We almost didn't beat them."

"Don't let Milton hear you say that," Thomas said.

"I wouldn't. Obviously."

# PIERCEHAVEN

"So how about if you just focus on Valley right now, and not worry about Rangeley yet?"

"Because Milton is already 'Rangeley this, Rangeley that.' He's freaking out."

"I'm sorry." Emily didn't know what else she could say.

And it wasn't just Chloe. She could see the stress etched in each of the player's faces. Not one of them looked healthy that week. Of course, the weather could've had something to do with it. The infamous winter had finally sunk its talons into Piercehaven, with wind chills ranging from ten below to thirty below. The thermometer in Emily's car that morning had read negative fifteen, and when she got out of the car, she had to walk into the wind to reach the school door, and for a moment was worried she wouldn't make it without dying.

As she graded poems from her creative writing students, she wondered if it was possible for an entire island to have seasonal affective disorder. Later, she mentioned that thought to James, who said, "You haven't seen anything yet. The island still has basketball. Wait till March."

Emily had to host two Valley students, so she had to go to the games. She probably would've gone anyway, especially since the gym/cafeteria was so much warmer than her house.

She hadn't asked James to go to the Seacoast Christian games with her, as she was still kind of stunned by his response to her invitation to the Camden Christian game, but she was feeling a little braver this week, and she did invite him to the Valley games.

And much to her surprise and delight, he accepted.

He even came to pick her up, and they went to the game sort of acting like a couple. The gym was, of course, packed, and she was elated to be able to sit smushed up against James's warmth. She was also elated to learn that James was not, unlike seemingly every other island resident, a screaming fanatical fan at basketball games. He sat there quietly watching, even though it was a close game. The only thing he said during the whole first quarter was, "Wow, this might be quite a barn burner," and he said it mostly to himself.

The first quarter ended with the score tied at eight. These were not the same girls she'd seen play before. They were still talented of course, but they seemed unfocused, almost frantic. Each starter had made a turnover in the first quarter, and Hailey already had two fouls, a fact that almost sent Milton into cardiac arrest. He had benched her and put junior Hannah Philbrook in. Someone behind Emily had said, "Oh, no, Milton, don't put *her* in. She's too slow." Then the other side of that conversation had said, "She certainly has chunked up this year." Emily was mortified, and prayed that Hannah's parents were nowhere nearby.

Hailey was back in during the second half, and she scored two quick hoops to get them ahead. But then she was called for another foul, and taken out of the game again. The fans went ballistic, many of them screaming obscenities at the refs. Emily wondered how much refs got paid. She figured however much it was, it should be more. She leaned toward James. "Was that really a foul?" she asked. James shook his head. This time, Milton put Victoria in, and she looked terrified.

At the end of the half, Piercehaven Lady Panthers were down by six points.

Emily and James stood to stretch, but didn't abandon their spots, for fear of losing them.

"I'd like to be a fly on the wall in that locker room," Emily said.

"No. You wouldn't," James said.

"How can he get away with hollering at them like that?" she whispered.

"Shh." Then, as if only trying to redirect her, "Would you like a hot dog or soda?"

"No, thank you." She didn't want anything. Plus, the concessions line stretched out into the hallway.

Minutes later, the girls returned to the court to deafening applause. No one had any doubt about their Lady Panthers. They would get it together in the second half.

Only they didn't. Jasmine traveled on the first possession.

On the second possession, Hailey scored, but was called for a charge. Her fourth foul.

"Did she foul that time?" Emily whispered.

"I don't think so," James said. "I'm not sure what these refs are up to, and I'm a little concerned about where they're sleeping tonight."

"People wouldn't actually harm the refs, would they?"

"Harm, I don't think so. Harass? I'm pretty sure."

"Is that why the Sheriff's here?"

"Among other reasons, yes."

"He's always here?"

"For every game, yes."

"Always the same guy?"

"He's the only cop in town, remember?"

"Isn't that kind of dangerous? What if he needs to call for backup?"

James looked at her. "Not much happens around here."

"Has anyone ever actually tried to assault a ref at a basketball game?"

"Of course."

The Valley point guard brought the ball up the floor, closely guarded by a red-faced MacKenzie. At the top of the key she made a quick pass out to the wing and then cut for the hoop. MacKenzie got caught by a screen, leaving the point guard wide open under the hoop, where she scored.

Milton was on his feet. "MacKenzie!" he screamed.

Chloe grabbed the ball and inbounded it to MacKenzie, who headed back up the court.

"MacKenzie!" Milton screamed again. "You wanna tell me when you're going to start playing in this game?" His voice cracked on the word game, and in that second, MacKenzie stopped walking and looked at him.

Chloe ran by her, leaving her alone, suspended halfway between the baseline and half-court, just standing there, dribbling, her face deadpan. The gym became eerily silent.

There was only the slap, slap, slap of ball against cafeteria tile.

Emily ripped her eyes away from MacKenzie's face so she could look at Milton. He stood still, hands on hips, glaring at her. It was a terrifying staring contest, and it made Emily physically sick to her stomach. She looked back at MacKenzie, who looked at the ceiling, still expressionless.

"She's only got ten seconds to get across half court," James muttered.

"Let's go!" someone shouted from behind them.

MacKenzie stopped her dribble then.

"Get on her!" the Valley coach cried out, his words echoing in the silent gym.

A Valley player ran toward MacKenzie, but MacKenzie stuck one hand out, using the same commanding presence she used on her own teammates, and the Valley player stalled.

"I said, get her!" the Valley coach repeated, but his players didn't move.

Every eye in the gym was on young MacKenzie. Every eye watched her lower the arm she'd used to halt the defense. Every eye watched her bend over and calmly set the ball on the floor. And every eye watched her turn and walk, calmly, her shoulders and chin high, the length of the court and out the gym doors.

173

# PIERCEHAVEN

Chloe was the first to move. She sprinted toward the ball, jolting the Valley player into action, who raced her there, but Chloe beat her out, dove on the ball, and immediately called for a timeout, which was granted.

At first, still no one else moved, and then both coaches called their players off the floor. Emily started to stand up, but James caught her hand and pulled her back down. "What?" Emily asked.

James nodded across the gym, at MacKenzie's mom, who was extricating herself from the bleachers.

"What just happened?" Emily breathed.

"Not sure. But I think our little MacKenzie just took a stand."

# Chapter 26

The Lady Panthers fell to 10 and 1.

James went to center court to help Emily locate her guests. MacKenzie's mom came back into the gym, breathless, with eye makeup smeared all over her face.

"Is she all right?" Emily whispered to her.

Heather forced a smile and nodded.

The Valley coach passed out his players, and Emily got Anna and Gabbie. The girls followed Emily and James out to his truck and wordlessly climbed in.

James started the truck and waited for a chance to pull out into the flow of traffic. Emily turned around and looked at the girls, crammed into the extended cab. "I just want you to know that I'm an English teacher, and I don't care a hoot about basketball."

The girls smiled, and though it was difficult to tell in the dark, Emily thought they also appeared to relax a bit.

"Also, congratulations on your victory."

The next morning, Emily was actually eager to get to the gym, a feeling she wasn't used to. She wanted to see MacKenzie. She'd prayed for her quite a bit the night before, and mostly expected her to have recovered from whatever it was that had happened last night.

But MacKenzie wasn't there.

Neither was her mother.

Chloe, looking exhausted, took the helm at point guard, and Victoria took over Chloe's spot. But if one didn't know these changes had been made, one wouldn't have been able to tell. The girls still functioned like one fine-tuned machine. Chloe was nearly flawless at point, and Hailey couldn't miss. On the rare occasions that she did, Lexi or Jasmine scooped up the rebound and put it back up and in. The half ended with the Panthers leading by 14 and everyone wondering how the night before had even happened.

MacKenzie came to church the next morning, and for the first time, her mother came with her. Emily wanted to talk to her, to give her support, but she wasn't sure what to say. So, after the service, she simply asked, "Are you OK?"

MacKenzie gave her a huge smile. "Oh, I am *so* OK. I've never been better."

"Did you quit the team?"

Her mom came to her defense then, throwing an arm around her shoulder. "We don't know yet."

"It's OK, Mom," MacKenzie said. "It's just Miss Morse. She doesn't care about basketball."

"Oh," Heather said, visibly relaxing. "Sorry, I'm just afraid of the fallout from this."

"Well, MacKenzie, and you, have my complete support. You can always come hide out in my room if you need to."

"I'm actually thinking of homeschooling her."

"Mom, don't be crazy—" MacKenzie said.

Heather shushed her with a stern eye.

"Well, know that if she's in school, I'll be keeping an eye out for her," Emily said.

"Thank you," Heather said, "and I mean that."

"Can you believe it?" Thomas asked as soon as Emily walked through her classroom door.

"I can," Emily said.

"Milton is soooo mad," Chloe said. "He says he's not going to let her back on the team this year, no matter what."

"I don't think that's going to be a problem," Emily said.

"Why?" Chloe asked.

"Nothing."

"No," Thomas said. "What? You know something we don't know." He looked so eager, Emily wondered if he was salivating.

"I don't know anything. I just wouldn't be surprised if MacKenzie doesn't want back on the team. That's all."

"Well then she has lost her mind," Chloe said.

# Chapter 27

Emily had just dropped her purse in her bottom drawer when her intercom buzzed. "Emily?"

Emily tried to hide her annoyance that Julie was calling her by her first name while Chloe and Thomas were in her classroom. Of course, Julie didn't know they were in her classroom before school had even started.

"Yes?"

"Mr. Hogan would like to see you."

Emily looked at the clock. "Now?"

"Yes." The intercom clicked off.

Emily peeled off her winter coat.

"Are you in trouble?" Thomas asked. He was smirking. He obviously didn't think she was in trouble, but Chloe's face was pale.

"No, I'm not in trouble. Be right back."

Emily weaved her way through the hallway toward the principal's office. There weren't very many kids in the school, but apparently every one of them was between her and Mr. Hogan. When she finally got to his office, his door was open. This was strange. His door was never open. She knocked on it anyway. He nodded an invitation and then motioned for her to close the door behind her. A lead ball settled somewhere low in her stomach.

"Yes?"

"Have a seat."

She sat.

"I'll cut to the chase." He leaned forward in his chair, his forearms resting on the top of his desk, his hands folded neatly together.

Emily tried to comfort herself by acknowledging that he didn't look menacing. Only tired. It didn't work. "OK," she said, her voice only a little shaky.

"It's come to my attention that you have been prophesying the students."

Emily's brows scrunched together involuntarily. "I'm sorry, *what*?"

"Have you been trying to convert your students to Christianity?"

She thought she understood then. "Oh, you mean proselytizing?" He pursed his lips then and she regretted the clarification. "Sorry, I wasn't trying to correct you. I was just trying to understand."

"And do you? Understand?"

She forced herself to think before speaking, but her mind was a swirling jumble of a thousand defenses trying to force their way out. "No, I don't, exactly, but I can tell you that I haven't been proselytizing anyone."

He didn't look convinced.

"Is this about Milton?"

His eyebrows flew up. "Why do you ask that?"

"Because he apparently told one of his girls not to talk to me anymore. Look, Mr. Hogan, I don't want to waste time with this. My faith is a huge part of who I am, it's true. In fact, I became a teacher *because* of my faith, because I wanted to help young people, but I also respect the boundaries of this job, and don't want to put myself, or you, or this school in an uncomfortable position." She waited for him to respond. When he didn't, she added, "I do go to church on the island, and there are students who go to church with—"

"The 'church' that meets in Abe Cafferty's basement?" He couldn't possibly have sounded more sarcastic when he spoke the word "church."

She smiled. She couldn't help it. She was proud of their subterranean flock. "That's the one."

"We do have a real church on the island, you know."

Again, she forced herself to think carefully before replying, and she felt the Holy Spirit suggest she not reply at all. So she sat there, trying not to look defensive.

"It would be completely inappropriate for you to try to force your religious beliefs on any student here."

"I understand."

"And while I can't stop you from going to the basement church, I would also suggest you consider the cost."

This confused her, and her face showed it.

"What I mean is, some people find it odd to forego a perfectly good community church to meet with a bunch of radicals in a basement. People may make unpleasant assumptions about you because of your associations."

She bit her tongue. Literally. She had to bite it in order to keep quiet. There was so much she wanted to say to this man.

"But for now, let's just focus on the accusation at hand. I will make a note in your file, and don't forget that your current contract is only good for one year. Not only can we terminate it at any time, for any reason, in fact, we don't even have to give a reason, but if you want to be invited to teach here next year, I suggest you take these allegations seriously."

"Yes, sir."

He stared at her. She stared back.

"You may go."

As she stood to leave, he added, "We may be a remote school, Miss Morse, but we are not some missionary project."

"Yes, sir," she said, when what she wanted to say was, "Sir, every school in America is a mission field."

Thomas was champing at the bit when Emily returned to her classroom, but she told him nothing. She did, however, put a hand on Chloe's shoulder and whisper, "Everything's fine. I promise."

She only partly believed this. In the big picture, she knew that God was in control, and that to be fired from a teaching job for allegedly speaking Jesus' love would actually bring her blessing. But on the small scale, the idea terrified her. She didn't want the embarrassment of such drama. She didn't want to be fired from anything, let alone her first real teaching job—she had never *failed* at anything. And most importantly, she didn't want to have to leave James. She couldn't imagine staying on an island that had fired her, and she knew James would never leave the island. So she fervently hoped that this would all blow over and she would keep her job.

# Chapter 28

The Panthers played at Rangeley the following weekend, but Emily didn't give the away games an ounce of thought. Even when she entered the hallway on Monday morning and found the place as somber as a morgue, she still didn't connect the dots.

She wondered who had died, and tried not to gawk at all the long faces as she made her way to her classroom. Confident that Chloe and Thomas would be waiting for her, as they always were, she opened her door to find only Thomas.

She started to shut the door behind her, so she could ask him for the scoop in private, then thought better of it and left the door open. She knew better than to put herself in a situation that might look anywhere near suspicious.

With only a glance at Thomas's face, she could see that whatever had sobered the kids in the hall wasn't affecting him. "What's going on out there?" she whispered.

He cocked a cocky eyebrow. "You didn't hear?"

She rolled her eyes. "If I had heard, I wouldn't need you, my spy, now would I? Now spill it."

He laughed. "The girls lost to Rangeley."

She let out a long breath. "Is that all? Didn't we know that might happen? Where's Chloe?"

"I don't know where Chloe is, and no, as far as I know, people didn't think it would happen, and Miss M, you should know … *everyone* is blaming MacKenzie."

"MacKenzie? She wasn't even there, was she?"

"Exactly. They're all saying that if she hadn't quit, they wouldn't have lost."

"Oh well."

"No, Miss Morse, you're acting like it's not a big deal. It *is* a big deal. Everyone on the island *hates* MacKenzie right now. This loss is going to put us in *third* place!" He added that last part as if it were the most horrifying development of all.

"OK, well, we'll just have to look out for her. Have you seen her today?"

"No. If she's lucky, she won't come to school today."

"Chloe's coming, isn't she?"

As if on cue, Chloe walked through the door. "Yeah, yeah, I'm coming. I'm late because I was talking to MacKenzie."

"You're not late," Emily said.

"Well, I'm not early because I was talking to MacKenzie."

"Is she OK?" Emily asked.

"Yeah, actually. Her mom doesn't want her coming to school today, but she seems to be fine. I actually think she's enjoying this a little."

"*Enjoying* it?" Thomas sounded horrified.

"Yeah, well, you know, she's kind of like, *well maybe they should have appreciated me more when they had me.*"

Thomas made an irritated, and irritating, *pfft* sound and crossed his arms over his chest.

"How about you, Chloe?" Emily asked. "Are you OK?"

"I'm not great." She plopped down into a chair. "I played fine the first night, and we beat them easy—"

"Easily," Emily interjected.

"Easily. Whatever. Anyway, but then I guess their coach is some kind of genius, because she figured out how to stop us. Well, stop *me*, anyway. They put on this wicked press and I just couldn't get the ball up the court. I had like ten turnovers in the first half. I thought Milton was going to kill me. But they weren't all my fault. No one would come get the ball, or no one *could* come get the ball. Finally, Hailey came to help me, and together, we could break the press, some of the time."

Emily only understood part of what she was saying, but she nodded empathically throughout the story. "Chloe, you did your best, and that's all anyone can do."

"It's MacKenzie's fault," Chloe said. "I mean, I get that she's my sister in Christ now, but man, she really burned us."

Emily was stunned. "Is that why you went to talk to her this morning? To give her grief?"

"No, I went to beg her to come back on the team! I'm not a point guard!" she said, as if her being a point guard was the most preposterous thing she'd ever heard. "We need her! She needs to snap out of whatever she's going through and get back on the team."

"Would Milton even take her back?" Thomas asked.

"Of course. All Milton cares about is winning. He'd make her run like a zillion suicides and then welcome her back with open arms."

"Suicides?" Emily repeated.

But Chloe ignored her. "Rangeley already beat Valley twice. That means we're going to face Rangeley in the Southern Maine finals. That means we need MacKenzie."

"How could you possibly know whom you're going to face already?"

Chloe looked at her as if she were stupid. "Because number one team plays eight. Rangeley will beat whoever that is, probably one of the Christian schools. Then we'll be either two or three, which means we'll beat either seven or six, and then we'll beat three, and then we'll have to play the winner of the other bracket, which I promise you, will be Rangeley."

Emily had no idea what had just been explained to her.

"But you split with them, correct? So didn't you come out even?"

"No, because we beat them first, and then they beat us, so they get their Heal points back."

"What?"

The bell rang. Emily was relieved.

"You don't have to understand," Chloe said, a little patronizingly. "Just trust me. I don't want to go to the playoffs without MacKenzie. I can't face that press again."

Unsure what a press even was, Emily said, "I'm sure that you can. Milton knows what he's doing, right? He'll prepare you."

As the freshmen filed into Emily's room, Chloe leaned forward and lowered her voice. "He is wicked smart, but they are *good*."

"I'll pray about it. You pray about it. You'll be fine. It *is* only a game, you know."

Chloe rolled her eyes. "Yeah. Right."

Thomas gave Emily a fist bump and then trotted out of her room.


When Emily walked into the teacher's room to retrieve her salad from the fridge, the three teachers who'd been chatting in a small group looked at her and then promptly left.

Kyle was sitting at a table, reading the paper.

"Was it something I said?" she asked. She was completely kidding.

His expression as he folded the paper told her the dramatic exit was no kidding matter. "Did Mr. Hogan talk to you?"

"About?"

"Oh don't play coy. About your Jesus fetish."

"He's not a fetish. And yes, he talked to me."

"Good." He stood up.

"Good? Why's that good?"

"Because I don't want you to get clotheslined by this. If you're going to be hanged, you should know it's coming. Give you time to prepare, and maybe dodge the garrote?"

"The garrote? What are you talking about?"

He came over to her then, stopping only a foot in front of her. "I don't think you're doing anything wrong, Emily, but new teachers, they have it rough here. If someone has decided they don't like you, as Milton apparently has decided, they will *find* a reason to get rid of you. Apparently, the reason they're going to use with you is Jesus."

"Milton? Milton hasn't given me any trouble in weeks."

"That's because he's afraid of your boyfriend."

Emily felt her cheeks flush. But her heart also skipped at someone calling James her boyfriend. *Was* he her boyfriend? "Did James do something to Milton?"

"I have no idea," Kyle said quickly, suddenly acting as if he was above such matters. "I'm just saying, the other teachers might distance themselves from you, to avoid the fallout."

"But not you?"

He smiled, and it was a charming smile indeed. "No, not me. I know how this island works, and I'm not scared. Besides, I'm on continuing contract. They'd have to work pretty hard to fire *me*."

# Chapter 29

MacKenzie came to school on Tuesday. The first chance she got, Emily whispered, "You doing OK?"

MacKenzie nodded enthusiastically. "Actually, I wanted to talk to you about something. I've been reading my Bible, and I'm like, super confused. Do you think I could bring you a list of questions, maybe during lunch, and you could explain them to me?"

Emily resisted the urge to shush her. She took a deep breath and said, "Of course. Anytime."

"I mean, I've Googled the verses I don't understand, but the Bible websites use big words, and every website says something different." Her face became serious all of a sudden. "I just really want to understand."

Emily felt guilty for thinking about her job in that moment and nodded. "I'll help however I can. But when I asked if you were OK, I meant about basketball."

MacKenzie tipped her head back. "Yeah, totally. I mean, some of the girls are being … are being words I shouldn't say, and that hurts a little, but I also don't care. I mean, I guess on some level, I knew they weren't really my friends, and I think Milton is telling them to try to pressure me back on the team. But really, I don't *want* to go back on the team. I'm so much happier now. I've got so much *time* now." She looked around and then whispered, "I started *karate!*"

Emily didn't understand why this was a conspiratorial topic. "Oh?"

MacKenzie laughed. "Yeah, my mom's actually going to take me to the mainland twice a week. Isn't that awesome? I've always wanted to do karate, but of course, Milton would never have let me."


James took Emily out to dinner that Thursday. She was as nervous as ever, and changed four times. It was ten below zero outside, without the wind chill factor, and her thin-walled house was freezing cold. Her two cats were huddled together in front of the woodstove. So she looked more like she was going snowmobiling than on a date, but she didn't think she had another choice. It was either bundle up or frostbite.

James greeted her on her front step with a peck on the cheek, which wasn't unusual, and a "You look beautiful," which was *highly* unusual.

Unsure how to respond, she finally said, "Thank you," but the thanks came so long after the compliment that she cringed at the awkwardness.

He held her hand as they walked to the running pickup in her driveway, and he opened the door for her, and then smiled as she climbed in. As he climbed in the other side, he said, "Cold enough for ya?" sounding about fifty years older than he was.

"Wouldn't be bad if I never had to go outside."

"Did you lose power last night?"

"Of course. Didn't the whole island?"

"Yep."

He sounded nervous, which made her more nervous. They rode the rest of the short trip in silence.

It was approximately eighty degrees inside the restaurant, and Emily was starting to regret her many layers. Then, after they had ordered their beef, James said, "Can we talk?" which made her blush, which made her feel even hotter. She pushed up her sleeves and pulled down on her collar.

"Of course." She rummaged through her purse until she found a pencil. She twirled her hair into a pile and then jammed the pencil through it to create a large makeshift bun.

James waited for her to finish before continuing. "I was just wondering what your plans are for next year."

"Next year?" She didn't know what to say.

"Right. Next year. I'm wondering what will happen if you don't have a teaching job next year. Any chance you'll stay on the island?"

She stared at him, her eyebrows squished together. "James, am I getting fired?"

"I didn't say that! It's just a question, Emily. Don't go getting all dramatic."

"Dramatic? I'm not getting dramatic! You just said I might not have a job next year, and you don't expect me to react to something like that?"

"Emily"—he took a deep breath—"I didn't say that. I'm just asking. What if you didn't teach here next year? That's all."

Emily didn't know what to say. She wanted to say, "Are you asking me to stay, because if you are, of course I would stay. I want to marry you and make little non-basketball-playing island babies. Maybe they could start a school band. Or poetry club." But she didn't say that, of course. She didn't want to scare him, and she didn't know why he was asking the question.

Apparently annoyed by her silence, he leaned back in his chair. "You know what, never mind."

She took a shaky breath and leaned forward, trying to regain what had been lost. "I would stay on this island for you, James. If you wanted me to. But I'm also feeling a little, OK, a lot, of pressure at work. Principal Hogan talked to me—"

"About what?"

"Someone complained about me, probably Milton—"

James made a noise that sounded a lot like a growl. "It wasn't Milton."

"How do you know that?"

"I just do. What? What did Hogan say to you?"

"He said that someone had told him that I was sharing the gospel with students."

"He said that?" James looked incredulous.

"Well, he didn't use those words, but yeah, he accused me of evangelizing."

"What did you say?"

"I denied it."

"You did?" Now he looked appalled.

"I didn't deny *Jesus*. I just denied preaching at school, which I don't ... usually."

He smirked.

"Now it's your turn," she said. "What do you know?"

"I don't know much. But it wasn't Milton. It was a parent. Not sure who."

"And?"

"And that's all I know. Some parent complained to someone, who mentioned something to Hogan. It was probably a basketball parent. MacKenzie is not being quiet about her newfound faith, which is great, but someone might connect the dots."

"What dots?"

"New teacher shows up, student connects with her, student goes to her church, student finds Jesus, student quits basketball, student claims to be happier than she's ever been."

"That's not the way it happened, and you know it!"

"Of course I know it, but it doesn't matter a lick *how* it happened. What matters is what people *say* happened."

"That's not fair!"

"No kidding. And if MacKenzie wasn't the starting point guard, this wouldn't be as big of a deal." He paused and leaned forward again, his face now only inches from hers.

198

She had an overwhelming urge to grab his face and kiss him madly.

"So, you know what you should do now?"

*Marry you and make babies?* she thought. "No, what?" she said.

"You need to start evangelizing their top scorer. Get Hailey saved. That would really get their goat." He sounded completely serious, but his eyes were dancing.

# Chapter 30

The Lady Panthers finished their regular season 16 and 2 and in third place—not too shabby for any other school in the state. The girls were devastated. The boys' team went undefeated, and took every chance to rub the girls' faces in it. When this happened, the girls blamed MacKenzie.

MacKenzie didn't seem to care. She had replaced basketball with karate—and Noah. At first, it seemed they were just friends, just Jesus pals, but it soon became evident that there was more to it than that. Noah walked around school with a new glow, and MacKenzie was positively swooning.

On the morning of February 15, three days before February vacation and basketball playoffs, MacKenzie and Noah met Emily at the door to her classroom.

"Good morning!" Emily said brightly, sincerely delighted to see two of her favorite young faces.

The enthusiasm wasn't reciprocated.

"What's wrong, guys?"

MacKenzie swallowed, then looked at Noah, who nodded solemnly. MacKenzie looked at Emily again. "I need to talk to you."

"Of course, come on in."

MacKenzie looked into the classroom, where Thomas and Chloe sat staring out at them.

"Alone?" MacKenzie added.

"OK." Emily looked at Thomas and Chloe. "Sorry, guys. Can you give us a minute?"

Chloe got up silently, but then looked at MacKenzie suspiciously as she walked past. Thomas made a big show of groaning about his displacement, but went willingly enough. Emily, MacKenzie, and Noah entered the classroom, and Noah shut the door behind them. Emily glanced back at him in surprise. He looked both terrified and determined.

"What is it, guys? You're freaking me out."

MacKenzie looked at Noah again. He nodded again. MacKenzie took a deep breath. "So, I think I know something. Actually, I know that I know it. And I told Noah, and he"—she looked at him again for reassurance, which he provided—"insisted we tell someone. And well, we couldn't think of anyone else to tell."

Emily took off her coat and hung it beside her desk. Then she sat down and looked up at them. "Why don't you guys sit down?"

MacKenzie sat on the other side of the desk. Noah stood behind her and put his hands on her shoulders.

Emily felt impatience welling up inside her. "Well?"

"You might think I'm crazy, but Milton is"— her voice cracked and she suddenly looked scared. Noah squeezed her shoulders— "Milton is sleeping with Lexi."

Emily was certain she had misunderstood. She knew Milton was something of a slimeball, but this?

"He's having sex with her. Has been, for I don't know how long." MacKenzie paused. "You don't believe me, do you?"

"Hang on." Emily held up a hand. "Just give me a second to absorb this. I don't *not* believe you. I just need a second to process. This is a serious accusation, and if it's true, which I'm not saying it isn't, but if it's true, we need to respond wisely. First, how do you know this?"

MacKenzie looked over her shoulder at Noah. He nodded again. "She got drunk on Saturday night, after the Temple game, and she told me..." MacKenzie seemed to sense doubt from Emily. "Yes, I was at a party, but I wasn't drinking! And yes, she was drunk, but it's true—I *know* it is. I've had this feeling for a very long time that something wasn't right. I just didn't know for sure what it was. And it's not just Lexi. I think it might be Victoria too."

"Victoria?" Emily exclaimed. She was only a freshman. Lexi, a senior, was disturbing enough, but a freshman? Somehow that seemed way more horrific. And more than one girl? This was no inappropriate romance. This was something far darker. "Why do you think that about Victoria?"

"He treats her differently. Like he does Lexi. He touches her a lot. Rubs her shoulders. Whispers in her ear." MacKenzie shuddered. "If he's not sleeping with her yet, he wants to be."

"OK," Emily said.

"OK?"

"Yep. I'll tell who needs to be told."

"That's it?" MacKenzie looked hopeful.

"I'm sure that's not it. But that's where it will start."

"Will anyone know?"

Emily thought she might cry. "I'm afraid people will know. I hate for these girls to be embarrassed, but—"

"No, I mean, will people know that I'm the one who told?"

"Oh … yes. I think people will probably know that too." Emily leaned toward her students. "But, MacKenzie, you are not alone in this. You have done the right thing. Whether or not this is true, I need you to hear me on this. You have done the right thing." Emily looked into her eyes, trying to convey her absolute certainty of this fact.

MacKenzie held her gaze, but she didn't look convinced.

# Chapter 31

Emily asked the librarian to cover her first period class for a few minutes, and then headed toward Mr. Hogan's office. Lexi was alone at her locker, and Emily couldn't help but stare. Her first thought, which she was ashamed of, was that Lexi wasn't terribly attractive. She was tall, probably taller than Milton even, and broad. She looked more like a boy than a girl, and her short hair didn't add any femininity. Lexi looked up and caught Emily staring, and Emily tried to fake a smile. She knew she'd failed, though. She wondered if she should ask Lexi before she went to Mr. Hogan and essentially threw a bucket of chocolate yogurt at the fan, but she wasn't sure what to say, how to ask, or how to respond to Lexi's answer. So she kept walking, feeling ill-equipped for every facet of this scenario.

Mr. Hogan's office door was closed and locked. Emily asked Julie if she knew when he'd be back and Julie looked at the clock. "Don't you have a class right now?"

"Do you know when he'll be back?" Emily repeated, a little terser this time.

"I don't."

Wordlessly, Emily headed toward guidance. The door was shut. She knocked. "Come in," Mr. Babcock called out. She opened the door to find him and Sydney Hopkins—alone, in his office, with the door shut. Twenty minutes before, this detail wouldn't even have registered, but now it terrified her.

"I need to speak with you for a minute," Emily said, and could hear fear in her voice.

"I'm with a student right now," Richard said, with no little condescension.

Emily looked at Sydney. "I'm sorry, Syd." Then she looked at Richard. "This can't wait."

He heaved a big sigh. "Can you step out for a minute, Sydney? This won't take long."

She obliged. Emily shut the door. "A student just told me that Milton is sleeping with Lexi Smith."

Much to Emily's horror, Richard actually laughed. He leaned back in his chair and tipped his head back and laughed at the ceiling.

Emily's jaw dropped.

"Who told you that?"

"Apparently Lexi told a friend at a party on Saturday night."

"Lexi doesn't go to parties during basketball season. You must be mistaken."

Emily didn't know what to do. She was angry, scared, and felt helpless. "Even if it's not true," she said in a small voice, "it still needs to be looked into."

He slapped his leg. "I will do that. I will look into it for you. Now"—he pointed at the closed door—"could you send Sydney back in?"

On the way back to her classroom, the waterworks started. Emily ducked into the staff restroom to try to get a grip. She leaned on the sink and took several long, deep breaths. Then she began to pray. "God, give me wisdom here. I'm freaking out. If it's not true, I don't want to hurt Lexi, or Milton—OK, maybe I do want to hurt Milton, but I don't want to destroy the man's life. But if it's true, oh God, if it's true, we've got to do something."

It was a long morning. Emily fought tears, and nausea, every moment. She was jumpy and sweating profusely despite it being only sixty degrees in her room.

When Larry paused to lean on his broom in her doorway during second period and scolded her for sitting on her desk, she responded with much less grace than usual. "Do you mind? I'm trying to teach a class here."

He actually stepped into the room. "That desk is older than I am!" he said threateningly.

"Well then it's obviously strong enough to endure my sitting on it," she spat. "Now get out of my classroom!"

To her surprise, he left, and she tried to pick up where she'd left off with *Of Mice and Men*, but all the kids were laughing.

"Way to go, Miss M," Thomas said, offering her another fist bump.

She ignored it. "Sorry, I shouldn't have acted that way. I'm having a difficult day."

"Don't apologize," Hannah said. "He deserves it. He's rude to everyone, acts like he runs the place."

"Regardless, I didn't mean to be disrespectful—"

"So, about Lennie's mouse," Noah said, and gave Emily a knowing look.

"Yes, Noah, thank you. About that mouse …"

When Lexi walked into Emily's classroom for her fourth period class, Emily felt something within her snap. She stared at Lexi, trying to see something—anything—to indicate that the apple cart had at least been bumped, if not upset. But Lexi was acting completely normally, and every cell of Emily's body was certain that her guidance counselor hadn't said a word to anyone.

"If you'll excuse me, class, I'll be right back." Back to the library she went, and asked the librarian again to cover. Back down the hallway she went to the principal's office, which was still locked up tight. Julie still claimed no knowledge of Mr. Hogan's whereabouts. Back up the hallway she went. It was empty and silent now, save for the click of her heels and her taut breathing. She had never felt so tightly wound in her whole life. She opened the door to Kyle's empty classroom, entered, and slammed the door behind her.

Startled, he shut the laptop, making it clear he'd been doing something he wasn't supposed to do. "Most people knock!"

She took four quick strides across the room and then sat down across from his desk. "A student told me this morning that Milton is having sex with Lexi Smith. I went and told Richard, but he laughed at me, and he hasn't done anything. Mr. Hogan's nowhere to be found. What do I do? Is it up to me to call the cops?"

Kyle's eyes grew wider as she talked, but when she stopped for a breath, he flashed that dazzling smile at her. "First thing we're going to do is *calm down*."

She nodded. "OK, then what?"

He smiled again. "Seriously, Emily, take a breath. You look like you're about to have a stroke."

She took a breath. He didn't seem satisfied. She took another.

"Good. Now, listen to me. This rumor, or ones like it, have been going around for *years*. Literally *years*. When I was in high school, they were saying the same thing about Milton's dad. It's just island junk. Non-basketball people talk smack because they're jealous."

She stared at him for several seconds. "You're saying it's not true?"

"I'm saying it's not true."

She let out a burst of air, and realized that she'd just been told exactly what she wanted to hear. "The student who told me, she said that Lexi told her at a party."

"We don't know what Lexi really said, but even if she did say that, I wouldn't put too much stock in a hormonal teenager's drunken angst."

Emily put her head in her hands.

"Hey, it's OK. You've reacted exactly how you're supposed to react. If it were true, it would be pretty messed up, but really, it's not true. I guarantee it. I have known Milton forever. He's a neanderthal, but he's not a pedophile."

She peeked out through her fingers at him. "Has anyone ever looked into it?"

He shrugged. "Dunno. But if you push this, you're not going to help yourself any. Who told you?"

Emily didn't answer.

"Come on, Em. Who told you? Chloe? Thomas?"

Emily shook her head and stood up to go. "Doesn't matter, right? If it's not true?" She headed toward the door. "Thanks for your help."

"Anytime, but Em?"

She stopped to look at him.

"If it ever happens again, just tell the student to go straight to Mr. Hogan. Then it takes you out of the equation. Less stress, less mess."

Emily, dismissing this advice as soon as it was given, nodded as if she hadn't, and left the room. MacKenzie had told her because MacKenzie had trusted her, had felt comfortable telling her, or at least comfortable *enough* to tell her. Emily couldn't imagine MacKenzie going to Mr. Hogan with such a thing.

She paused outside her classroom, her hand on the doorknob. A lot of what Kyle had said had made sense, right? If it were true, surely there would have been signs. There's no secrets on an island, right? She decided that it must not be true after all.

But that night, she couldn't fall asleep. That night, she rolled over every ten seconds, pounded the pillow every fifteen, alternated between crying and hard-won self-control. She decided she needed to just ask Lexi, but then realized that, if it weren't true, how wildly inappropriate that would be. How it would make Lexi feel. What would happen to her job if Lexi told anyone. Which she would, because there are no secrets … or are there?

At two o'clock in the morning, Emily got out of bed and got dressed. She stepped out into the subzero weather and started her car. Then she drove to the small cape on the other side of the island, where she climbed out of her car and knocked on the door. Moments went by. She knocked again. A bright light came on directly above her head and blinded her.

The Sheriff opened the door in his pajamas. "Yes?"

"Sorry to bother you, Sheriff," she began, her voice shaking.

"What is it?"

She took a deep breath. "I'm a teacher at the high school—"

"I know who you are." He stepped out onto the porch, shutting the door behind him. "Don't you have a phone?"

"I do, but I didn't know your phone number."

"But you know where I live?"

"Someone showed me."

"Remind me to thank Gagnon for that.... Well, *what*?"

"A student told me today that Milton Darling is having an affair with one of our seniors, Lexi Smith."

The Sheriff stared at her expressionlessly.

She shifted her weight back and forth, trying to force some blood into her toes.

"Who?"

"Lexi Smith," she said, more slowly this time.

"No, I mean, who told you this?"

"Oh ... I don't think I'm ready to say."

He looked dumbfounded. "Not ready to say? What do you think this is? Someone levels an accusation like that? They don't get to stay anonymous."

"I understand. I just wanted to wait … to wait …" She wasn't sure how to finish her sentence.

"Wait for what?"

"Wait to make sure you're going to do something about it."

"What?"

Emily took a deep breath and the cold hurt her lungs. "I already told the guidance counselor, who laughed at me, so I'm not really confident that you're going to do something either. And if you're not, then I'd like to protect the student who told me. She told me because she was concerned about Lexi, not for any other reason."

The Sheriff leaned toward Emily, and she reflexively took a step back.

"Ma'am, if a child is being sexually assaulted, you can certainly know that I'm going to *do something. Now, what student told you this?*"

Emily didn't know what to do. Most of her just wanted to give up MacKenzie's name, but there was this small part of her that resisted. And it was this part, and her cold toes, that won the fight. She began to back away. "Just look into it? Please?" She continued backing toward her car, suddenly desperate to be within its relative safety and warmth. "If it's not

ROBIN MERRILL

true, no harm done, right? And if it's true?"
She got into her car and without another look,
backed out of the driveway and drove home.

She was asleep mere seconds after her
head hit the pillow.

# Chapter 32

Emily was a tangle of emotions the next morning. She felt one hundred percent confident she had done the right thing. But she was also one hundred percent terrified of the fallout. And it wasn't even about losing her job—that she could deal with. It was about the public spectacle this would all make, the shame, the pain it would bring.

Lexi was at her locker. Business as usual. *That's OK*, Emily thought. *Got to give him some time to act. Probably hasn't even had his coffee yet*. This thought cheered her, until she spotted Victoria at her locker. And Milton. He was standing at an angle, one arm draped over her open locker door, and his body blocking any means of escape. Not that she looked as though she wanted to escape. She didn't. She looked calm and content. But Milton was just standing *so close* to her. His posture made the hairs on the back of Emily's neck stand up. She thought of how she might intervene, but came up with nothing that wouldn't make a scene, and so she kept walking. As she did, though, she caught Noah's eye. He was watching her watch them.

She beckoned to him with a finger. He grabbed MacKenzie's arm, which was, of course, mere inches from his own, and they followed Emily down the hall.

She stopped outside her room, because she knew her regulars were already in there. "I told Mr. Babcock yesterday," she whispered to them. "But I don't think he did anything. I don't think he believed me." (This wasn't entirely accurate, but this was the version she would give the kids.) "So I told the Sheriff last night. I haven't given anyone your names—yet. I'll probably have to, but for now, no one knows who told me."

MacKenzie nodded. "Thanks, Miss M."

Emily nodded back. "Try to have a good day."

Emily did not have a good day. Her nerves stayed on edge and every time she saw Milton or Lexi or Victoria, her chest got so tight she wondered how she'd draw her next breath. She prayed silently all day long, and when she got home, she collapsed on her couch and prayed some more—till she fell asleep.

So she was unprepared when James knocked on her door at six.

She jumped off the couch and flung the door open. "I'm so sorry, James. I totally forgot about dinner. I fell asleep. Just give me two minutes, and I'll get ready. Come on in." She stepped back and held the door open, but he stood rooted to his spot. She rolled her eyes.

"I'll wait in the truck. No hurry. It's not like we have reservations."

She giggled, despite her annoyance at his strict adherence to his honor code. She enthusiastically watched his backside as he walked toward the truck, and then she shut the door. She ran upstairs, changed into something less schoolmarmy, tried to fix her makeup, and then wished she'd never looked in the mirror, before tearing back down the stairs.

Finally, out of breath, she climbed into his truck.

"I said you didn't have to hurry."

"I know, but I felt bad." She tried to smile at him.

"Isn't it felt badly?"

"Did you seriously just try to correct my grammar? And no, it's bad."

"Are you sure?" He backed out of her driveway.

She looked at him. "Of course I'm sure! If you 'feel badly,' you're doing a bad job of feeling your way across a dark room. If you have unpleasant emotions, you feel *bad*."

He laughed then, and she saw that he'd just been messing with her. This pleased her somehow.

"What's got you in a tizzy?" he asked.

"It's just … a lot's been going on."

"Such as?"

She began to tell him, but before she'd said six words, he yanked the truck over to the side of the narrow road and looked at her gravely.

"What?" she asked.

"Go on."

She told him everything.

"Why didn't you tell me?"

"I just did."

"Emily, why didn't you tell me *yesterday?* I could've helped!"

"Helped how? James, I'm sorry. I wish now that I had told you, but it honestly didn't occur to me. It's not like I tried to investigate myself. I just tried to get someone to listen to me."

"And did he?"

"Who, the Sheriff?"

James nodded.

"I don't know."

James gave a huge sigh.

219

"Can we go now? I'm hungry."

He nodded, and put the truck back in drive.

She waited until they were back on the road before asking, "Do you think it's true?"

He didn't answer at first, and then he looked at her. "I don't know."

This answer was the most damning evidence she'd heard yet. "You've known him a long time. Do you think he's capable of such a thing?"

He stared straight ahead, but she could see his jaw muscles moving. Then he gave the faintest shake of his head. "I wouldn't dare say."

She was getting a strong I-don't-want-to-talk-about-this-anymore vibe from James, but she couldn't help herself. "Kyle said that such rumors have been going around for years. Have you ever heard anything like this before?"

James made the grimace-face he always made at the mention of Kyle's name, and then said, "I heard things when I was in school, about Milton's father, but … but we were just kids. We thought it was a joke. I don't think any of us ever really thought anyone was being *abused*. Maybe that's what this is, just a continuation of that old story, but … but I just don't know." He looked at her then. "And why are you talking to Kyle about this and not me?"

"Because I was trying to get advice. I'd already told Mr. Babcock, and he didn't do anything, so I didn't know whom to go to next."

"And what did Kyle tell you to do?"

"He told me to calm down. He said it wasn't true."

"Typical."

"What's that mean?"

"It means Kyle's a fish. Always has been."

"A fish?"

"He's slippery."

# Chapter 33

When Emily pulled into the school parking lot on Friday morning, she saw Lexi, all bundled up by the door. By the time she opened her car door, Lexi was right there beside it.

"Good morning, Lexi."

"Miss Morse, please, you've got to stop. It's not true."

"OK, Lexi, let's go inside and talk. It's freezing out here."

"No, if we go inside, people will hear us. And we don't need to talk. You just need to stop trying to get Milton in trouble."

"Lexi, I'm not"—Emily put a hand on Lexi's arm, but she yanked it away—"trying to get Milton in trouble. If he's not hurting you, great, but if he is—"

"Of *course* he's not hurting me. He would never hurt me. And if you don't stop lying, he's going to find out, and he is going to be so mad." This came out like a threat.

For once, Emily wasn't scared of Milton. "Of

course he'll be mad. I don't care about that. I only care about you and the other girls."

"What other girls?" A different emotion flickered across her face, but Emily wasn't sure what it was. Surprise? Doubt?

"All of them. Coaches aren't supposed to be sexually involved with their athletes."

"He's not."

"OK, good. Now, I'm going inside. Come on. It's cold out here." She stepped around Lexi and went inside, leaving her standing in the cold.

It was the day before February vacation, and the energy in the hallway was palpable. That afternoon, all the students would be released for an entire week, though most of them—most of the entire island—would spend the week in Augusta.

Basketball divided the state into two regions: Southern and Northern. Each region spent the week battling it out to find a champion. Southern Maine fought these battles in Augusta, Northern Maine in Bangor. Then, each winning team would play one week later, in the state final game, which this year, would also be in Augusta.

That meant hours and hours in the Augusta Civic Center, in hard plastic chairs, eating too-spicy plastic cheese poured over too-salty tortilla chips and drinking not-fizzy-enough sodas. For much of the state, it was the high point of the entire year.

Lexi's parking lot outburst had led Emily to believe that the investigative process had been started, but as she walked by the main office, she saw Milton in there. And he was laughing. Four basketball players, including Chloe, stood around him, and they were all yukking it up.

She felt sick. She turned and walked back out into the cold. Her eyes scanned the parking lot, but no Lexi. She felt a small panic. Where had she gone? Maybe she shouldn't have left her alone—she'd been so upset. Then she saw her. Sitting alone in her car.

Emily headed that way. As she got closer, she could see Lexi was crying. She opened the passenger side door, and Lexi jumped. "May I get in?"

Lexi nodded.

She shut the door behind her. "I'm sorry, Lexi. For all of it. How did you know that I had told someone?"

She shrugged.

"If you want me to stop pushing, you need to talk to me. How did you know?"

She sniffed, and then wiped her nose on her sleeve. Emily started to dig through her purse for a tissue. "The Sheriff called my mom. She is *so mad* by the way."

"At me?"

"Yes, at you. Who do you think?"

Emily handed her a tissue, which she took without comment. Emily took a deep breath. "Your mom doesn't know?"

Lexi glared at her. "There's nothing *to* know."

Emily waited, carefully considering her next words. "Lexi, do you remember talking about this at a party last weekend?"

She shrugged.

"You told someone that this *was* true."

"You weren't there."

"Lexi, look at me."

She pointedly looked out the driver's side window.

"Lexi, I am on your side. I want to help you."

Her head whipped around. "You want to *help* me? Miss Morse, you are trying to *ruin* everything! My basketball career, my relationsh…" She didn't finish the word.

"Your relationship with Milton?"

A new sob wracked her body. "Miss Morse, I *love* him. And he loves me. Can't you understand that?"

Emily put a hand on her back. "I do

understand. And I'm so sorry. Does your mother know?"

Lexi shook her head. "Milton said we couldn't tell anyone, because people wouldn't understand." She glared at Emily. "He was right. Obviously."

"How long have you two been together?"

She shrugged. "Since sophomore year."

"You know what? Let's go tell your mom. Right now. I'll go with you. She needs to know."

Lexi's eyes grew wide. "No way! You don't even know my mother! Just stay out of my life!" Lexi flung open her door and threw herself out of the car. Then she ran into the school.

Silently cursing the lack of cell service for the thousandth time, Emily got out of the car and went into the school to find a landline. Once she did, she realized she didn't have a number to call. She had to walk the length of the building to get to her room to use her computer. The first bell had already rung, and kids were scurrying to their first class. She met Chloe and Thomas coming down the hall.

"You're late!" Thomas said in a mock-scolding voice. "Where have you been?"

"I'll tell you later!" she called, without slowing down. She blew into her room, dropping everything on the desk as she called out to her freshmen, "Happy Friday! Let's do a free write. Tell me what your plans are for this week."

"Tournaments, obviously," Victoria said.

"Right. Write about that," Emily said absently as her fingers typed "Maine State Police" into the search bar. She wrote down the number, told the class she'd be right back, and then went to ask the librarian to cover.

"I have my own job to do, you know."

"I know, thanks so much," Emily said and hurried toward the teachers' room.

Her fingers trembled as she dialed the number. An operator answered. Emily took a deep breath. "I'm calling from Piercehaven High School. A student has just told me that she is being sexually abused by a teacher here. Can you send—"

"Would you like to report a crime?" a snarky voice said.

Emily lost whatever shaky semblance of emotional control she had. "Yes, I would like to report a crime! Isn't that what I just said?"

"Hold please."

She was transferred to another voice, this one identifying himself as a police officer. She repeated her cry for help, and he told her he would have officers on the next ferry.

This should have comforted her, but it scared her. She hung up the phone with fingers that had suddenly gone cold. Maine State Troopers were coming on the next ferry. This was really happening. No turning back now. But that was good, right? This needed to happen. It would be ugly, but not as ugly as pretending nothing was happening. She smoothed out her skirt and headed back down the empty hallway to relieve the librarian.

# Chapter 34

Hannah joined her class halfway through second period. She had just returned from a dentist appointment on the mainland, and she had juicy news she just couldn't wait to share: "There were *four staties* on the ferry!" she blurted out as soon as she sat down.

Everyone started firing questions at her, everyone except Noah, who just looked at Emily knowingly.

Theories abounded. Lots of names were thrown out. Someone had died of suspicious causes. A big drug bust. Bojack had finally hit his wife too many times. Emily didn't know who Bojack was, and tried to rein the class back in, but it wasn't easy.

Only minutes after she had turned their attention back to the Neil Gaiman story in front of them, a State Trooper knocked on her classroom door. His commanding presence, so foreign to that space, had an E. F. Hutton effect on her students. They all just stared at him, as if they were watching the most exciting movie ever filmed.

"Sorry to interrupt," the officer said. "Could you please dismiss"—he consulted his notepad—"Hailey Leadbetter and Hannah Philbrook?" He looked at Emily. "I need to speak with them."

Emily nodded to him. Then she looked at her girls, who appeared frozen and glued to their seats. "It's OK, girls, go ahead."

Hailey looked at her with panic in her eyes. "Why are they here?"

Emily took a step toward her. "It's OK, Hailey. You're not in trouble."

"How do you know?" she said, but she gathered up her books and followed Hannah out of the classroom.

"What was that all about?" Thomas asked when they'd gone.

Noah looked at Emily. No one answered Thomas.

"No really," he insisted. "It's not OK that something is happening in this school and I don't know about it!" Everyone laughed then, and just like that, the blue-uniform-spell was broken.

After class, Kyle popped into the room. He walked right up to Emily and muttered, "Any idea why staties are pulling basketball players out of classrooms?"

She nodded.

He looked horrified. "You didn't."

She nodded again. "I had to, Kyle. Lexi admitted it. She told me the truth. He's a rapist."

She had whispered the words, but Kyle still shushed her and then, with disgust all over his face, turned on his heel and left the room.

Hailey returned for her third period AP class. She had clearly been crying. Unsure of what to say, Emily didn't say anything. She just began handing papers back. When she handed one to Hailey, Hailey looked up at her and said, "You just cost us states."

"There are things more important than basketball, Hailey," she said, more sharply than she'd intended. She was just suddenly so *sick* of all the basketball. How could a girl as smart as Hailey not see what really mattered here?

Jasmine joined them then. She too had been crying.

Emily shut the door. There were only four kids in this class, and they were all present: Hailey, Hannah, Jasmine, and Blake, the senior center on the boys' team. "Do we need to talk about this?" Emily asked.

No one answered at first.

Then Hannah said, "Not to you."

"Look, I don't care if you're mad at me. I honestly don't. I did the right thing."

Hannah glared at her. "So it *was* you?"

"You just said it was!"

"Yeah, but we didn't know for sure. It was really you?"

"Yes." Emily took a deep breath and sat at one of the student desks. "It was me. What would you have me do? He was committing a *crime*, Hannah. A crime against one of your teammates."

"You could've waited till the end of the season."

Emily couldn't believe Hannah had just said such a thing.

"How old is Mr. Darling?" Emily asked the group.

"Mr. Darling?" Hannah repeated with some snark.

"Yes, Mr. Darling. Your teacher. Your athletic director. Your coach. The grown adult who chose the profession of educating *children*, how old is he?"

Hannah shrugged. "Dunno."

"Well, how many gold balls has he coached?"

"Eight," Hailey said.

"OK, so that makes him at least ..." Emily paused to do some math, which wasn't her strong suit. "... thirty?"

Hannah shrugged again.

"It's not healthy or safe for a thirty-year-old man to be sexually involved with a fifteen-year-old girl."

"Lexi isn't fifteen," Hannah snapped.

"She wasn't talking about Lexi," Hailey said quietly.

Actually, Emily had been talking about Lexi, about a younger version of Lexi, but this new development was not good news. Emily resisted the urge to ask whom Hailey was thinking about. "Hannah, abusers rarely target only one victim. There is almost always more than—"

"Stop calling him an abuser! He's not an abuser!" She was verging on hysterical. "It's just an island thing. Older men date younger women all the time. You just don't understand!"

"Hannah," Hailey said softly, "stop. He is. He is an abuser."

It was quiet for a few seconds and then Blake put his hands up in the air. "I just want to say that I didn't know any of this was happening! I didn't even know the cops were here until I saw them taking Milton out in handcuffs."

Hannah put her head down on her desk. "They took him?" she mumbled into the desktop.

"Sorry, didn't mean to make it worse," Blake said. "I just meant, how does something like this happen without anyone knowing?"

"No one *wanted* to know," Hailey said, almost to herself.

"Did you know?" Blake asked her.

"No. I really didn't." Hailey looked around the room. "At least, I didn't think I knew. But then, when it was all out in the open, when it was all real, I realized that I did know ... I just didn't know exactly what I knew."

"You just made absolutely no sense," Blake said.

Ignoring him, Hailey added, "But we really are screwed for playoffs now."

Emily stood up. "Hailey, I don't know much about basketball, and even I can see that you are God's gift to the basketball court. You are an absolute miracle out there. I've never seen any young woman play like you, with the grace and intelligence and instinct you have. You don't need Mr. Darling, or anyone else for that matter. You just need to do your thing, and you'll be fine. You'll be better than fine. You'll be golden."

No one was angrier with Emily than Chloe. She stomped into sixth period and threw herself into her desk. Emily asked her if she was OK, and she refused to answer, or even look at her. Emily quickly tired of this and started to walk away.

Then Chloe spoke up: "He's innocent, you know."

Glenn snorted. "Yeah, right. That's why girls are accusing him of rape."

Emily held a hand up toward Glenn, in an effort to silence him.

"He didn't *rape* anyone!" Chloe shrieked.

"Chloe, they're not just going to throw Mr. Darling in prison. There's a process, one that will find out the truth. And if he's innocent, they will find that out."

"And then what?" Chloe snapped. "His life is ruined."

"If he's innocent, his life will not be ruined."

"He didn't do it, Miss Morse." She was pleading with her. "He didn't. I *know* him. I've known him my whole life. He could *never* do something like this."

# Chapter 35

Emily was called out of class during seventh period. It was her turn with the police.

"You're the one who called us?" A kind-voiced man named Officer Hemlock asked.

"Yes."

"Why didn't you identify yourself?"

"I didn't mean not to. I'm not trying to be anonymous or anything."

He nodded, writing something down on his notepad, and then said, "OK, why don't you start at the beginning. Just tell us what you know, and how you came by that information."

She told him everything. It took her longer than she'd expected. She didn't give him MacKenzie or Noah's name, and he didn't ask for them.

When she had finished, he asked, "And do you know anything about Mr. Darling's interactions with Victoria Smith?"

Emily felt sick. "No, not really. Is she a victim too?"

The officer didn't answer.

"But she's only a freshman."

"Yes, ma'am. You can go now. Thank you for your time."



Emily met James at the door on her way out of the school building.

"Hey!" she said, surprised and delighted to see him.

"Hey, yourself. You OK?"

"I'm fine. You didn't have to come down here to check on me."

He gave her a broad smile. "I'm not here to check on you. I'm here because they've asked me to take over Milton's job."

"Which one?" Emily asked, shocked.

"The coaching one."

"*You're* going to coach the girls' team? Why you?"

"Well, if you think about it, there are lots of reasons to ask me."

She followed him into the gym. "Such as?"

"Such as"—he sat down on the bleachers and began taking off his boots—"I was quite the player once upon a time, such as I have a good reputation on this island for not being a creep, such as I'm the only one who said yes."

"They asked other people before you?"

237

"I don't know. But I'm certainly assuming so. Now, I love spending time with you, but can you leave before the girls get in here? I think I'm going to have enough drama on my hands." He stood up.

She nodded, looked around the gym to make sure they were alone, and then gave him a kiss on the cheek.

"Why the quick scan?" he asked. "You embarrassed to kiss me in public?"

"Not at all," she said quickly, "but I'm kind of a pariah around here right now, and I didn't want to bring you down with me."

He grabbed her by the shoulders and gave her a real kiss on the lips, the first one ever. It was quick, firm, perfect, and left her head spinning. He pulled away. "A little late for that, don't you think?" He smiled.

She smiled back, both breathless and speechless.

"I'm proud of you," he said softly. "You did a good thing here. You were right, and you did the right thing. Now, get out of here."

She turned and practically floated out of the gym. He had kissed her on the lips. On the lips! This was such a good sign, not to mention a pleasant experience. And he had used the word love. He hadn't said he loved *her*, exactly, but he did say he loved spending time with her, and after the day she'd had, that was enough.

# Chapter 36

James called her that night. The ring, so rare a sound in her home, startled her. She found herself hoping it was him, and was relieved when it was.

"Were you planning on going to the game tomorrow?" he asked.

"I was."

"Would you like to ride the bus?"

"I guess? Can I do that?"

"Well … no. But I'd like to make you my assistant. Then you can. I would have invited you to ride in my truck like a normal person, but now that I'm the coach—"

"Your assistant? I don't know anything—"

"I know you don't know anything. I don't want you for basketball. I want you for emotional support. These girls, they're pretty shook up, and well, I'm just not very good with emotions."

"Of course. I'll be your assistant. But isn't that going to tick people off? Doesn't everyone hate me right now?"

"The girls don't hate you. I've heard them talking. They adore you. Well, Chloe is angry, but she'll figure things out. And anyone who hates you has something really wrong with them. The man is a predator. When the shock and embarrassment fades, I think people will be grateful for what you did. Maybe you'll even be a hero."

"Pfft! I doubt it. But sure, I'll be your assistant."

They had to catch the seven a.m. ferry, much to Emily's horror. James picked her up at six, while she was still trying to find something red to wear.

"Come in!" she hollered down the stairs.

She heard the door open.

"Be right down! I'm trying to find something red!"

"What?"

"Something red!" she hollered. "You know, school spirit?"

"You don't have to wear red!" he hollered back.

She started down the spiral staircase and saw that he hadn't even stepped inside. "It's

OK, I found a scarf." She looked at him. "Wow!"

He grinned. "Don't even start."

He was wearing dark jeans she hadn't seen before, a pressed white dress shirt, and a red tie. He looked amazing. But even more amazing was the fact that she was wearing almost the same exact thing. "We couldn't have planned this any better."

"Right. Come on, let's go. The island's waiting."

She had no idea what he meant, but it didn't take her long to find out. The crowd started nearly a half-mile away from the ferry terminal. Every vehicle on the island appeared to be parked along both sides of the narrow road, and people filled the road, all of them walking toward the ferry.

"What is this?" she asked.

"The sendoff."

"All these people are going on the ferry?"

"A lot of them, yes. Some folks went over last night and got hotel rooms. Some of them will catch the next ferry."

"Will they all fit?"

"They don't all bring cars. The school hires a spirit bus, which picks people up on the other side and takes them to Augusta. It'll shuttle 'em back and forth all week."

"You're pretty confident that we'll win this first game."

He looked at her. "We're playing Greenville. We'll be all right."

Emily clicked her tongue. "Cocky. So everyone on the island goes to Augusta, seriously?"

"No, but most of them do. Everyone else just watches on TV."

"The games are televised?"

"Of course. The whole state will be watching. This is a big deal, Em. It's not all just in their heads. Wait till you see these girls being interviewed on the news, the composure, the maturity ... you won't even believe it."

The ferry was packed. The girls were all in the same cabin, with James, Emily, and a few parents. The mood was sober. Chloe sat in a corner and looked to be grieving. She wouldn't look at or speak to Emily.

Occasionally a girl would laugh, or act excited, and would then look guilty and rein in her joy. When Hailey did this, Emily spoke quietly to her. "You're allowed to be happy, you know."

Hailey nodded. "I am. Happy. It's just ... a lot. I don't want to act happy with Lexi and Victoria here. And also, we miss him, even if

243

he was a creep. We all loved him and we miss him. There's like this absence. I believe that he did it, which some girls don't, but I do. But even still, I'm having a hard time remembering that I believe that. Does that make sense?" She looked at Emily and her eyes were almost pleading.

"It does make sense, and I wish you girls had a chance to process all this before heading into the playoffs. But I hope you can still enjoy this experience. Don't let him take it away from you."

"You know?" She laughed humorlessly. "I've actually wondered if he'll be able to watch the game from jail. I mean, even after all this, I still want him watching me. I want to impress him, to make him proud. Isn't that crazy?"

"No, honey. You're not crazy. You're a victim."

"I am not!" she snapped, and a few other girls looked at her.

"I didn't mean that kind of victim," Emily said quickly. "He may never have touched you, but he abused your trust, and he broke your heart."

She nodded, and a tear slid down her cheek.

"Sorry, didn't mean to make you cry again."

"It's OK. I've been crying pretty much right steady since yesterday morning."

"I'm so sorry, Hailey. I wish none of this would have happened. But know that you are an amazing young woman and you are going to shine through all this."

Hailey took a deep breath. "I hope so."

# Chapter 37

The girls stood in a hallway, silently lined up in their million dollar warmups. The boys' team stood in front of them, holding a giant papered hoop the girls would soon bust through to adoring roaring applause.

Some tired mom had painted "Mighty Panthers" on the giant paper circle.

Hailey stood in the front of the line, holding one ball.

Chloe stood just behind her, holding the other. Her face was as white as snow and she was breathing heavily. Emily eyed her closely. Chloe caught her watching and turned to her. "I can't do this," she cried out. Her voice cracked and she began breathing even more heavily. She bent over and rested her hands on her knees. "I can't, I can't, I can't."

Emily took three quick steps and gently grabbed her arm. "Stand up, Chloe."

Chloe stood.

"OK, time to go," James said from behind them.

"Just a second," Emily said. "Chloe, look at me." She grabbed her shoulders and made Chloe face her.

Chloe looked.

"You, my sweet girl, are a child of God. You have absolutely *nothing* to fear—"

"I can't do it. I can't. I'm not a point guard. I'm going to fall apart. I can't do this."

Emily shook her gently. "Chloe, listen! Take a deep breath."

Chloe just kept panting.

"Do it with me, Chloe. Breathe in ..." Emily inhaled deeply.

Chloe followed suit.

"Now breathe out." Emily exhaled.

Chloe exhaled.

"And again." Emily inhaled, vaguely aware that the entire team was staring at them. "Now keep breathing while I give you a word here. *You* are so much more powerful than you know right now. *You* are a child of God. *You* are a miracle. You don't have to do this on your own. God's not going to leave you out there on your own. Do you hear me?"

Chloe nodded.

"OK, pray with me right now." She bowed her head. "And keep breathing. Father, these

# PIERCEHAVEN

girls have been through so much, but you know their precious hearts, God. Help them to remember who they are right now, that they are so much more than this present situation. Reach out and touch your daughter, Chloe. Take away her anxiety. Take away her fear and replace it with confidence. Confidence in you, God. Help her to focus on the task at hand, so that you may be glorified. In Jesus' precious name, amen." She picked her head up to see that the entire team had been bowing their heads as well. "OK, girls, go get 'em."

Chloe looked at Emily. Her eyes were wet, but her breathing was normal again. "Thank you," she whispered.

"You're welcome."

"You heard the woman," James said. "Let's go have some fun."

Hailey made a satisfying crashing noise as she busted through the paper, and Chloe was right on her heels, her chin held high. And the entire stadium erupted in applause.

Emily and James did not run out through the hoop, but much to her surprise and delight, he did take her hand in his before he led her out onto the floor and to the bench, which wasn't really a bench at all, but a long line of sturdy plastic chairs.

"You don't even look nervous," she said.

"I'm not."

"How is that possible?"

"Because this really has nothing to do with me. If we lose, which we won't, everyone will blame the situation. If we win, great. Everyone's happy. If we lose, which we won't, the girls finally get to take some time off and process all this."

"You must be more competitive than that, though."

He looked at her. "I used to be. But I'm not anymore. It's just a game."

Emily looked up at the crowd and her breath caught. First of all, the stadium was bigger than she'd remembered. She'd been there years before for a TobyMac concert, but now, with all the lights on, the place looked cavernous, completely dwarfing the hardwood basketball court at its center. Second, nearly half the arena was bathed in red and white—as if millions of candy canes had been crushed up and sprinkled everywhere. She giggled at the hundreds of red and white pompoms.

"What?" James asked at her laugh.

"Just the pompoms. We don't even have cheerleaders. Where did those come from?"

"Not sure, but they manage to come back every year."

Emily spotted MacKenzie near the front. They made eye contact and Emily gave her a little wave, wondering if she was regretting her decision, hoping she was not.

Emily sat down on the bench and watched the girls warm up. They looked good, all things considered, but what Chloe had gained in confidence, Victoria had apparently given up. Emily began to pray for her, and before she was emotionally ready, the buzzer sounded. Warmups were over.

Warmups came off. Names were announced. Hands were shook. National anthem was played. And then it was time. Emily's gut was full of knots. She couldn't believe how much pressure these girls—these *kids*—underwent.

The starting five trotted out onto the floor.

Emily sat down next to Victoria. "You OK?"

Victoria looked at her wide-eyed and shook her head. "I am so not OK." She lowered her voice. "Everyone *knows*." Emily didn't respond right away, so Victoria clarified, "Everyone knows what I *did*."

"May I touch you?" The question surprised Emily even as she asked it, but Victoria nodded, and Emily put a hand on her back.

"Victoria, *you* did not *do* anything. What happened is *not your fault*. And yes, some people know, but a lot of people don't, and a lot of people never will, because everyone is caught up with their own drama. Junk happens in this life. I'm sorry so much of it is happening to you right now, but you *will* get through this. I promise."

Victoria nodded. "I don't want to play. Can you tell James that I don't want to play?"

"Sure. I'll talk to Mr. Gagnon for you."

Hailey scored and the crowd behind the bench erupted. They had only just calmed down when Hailey stole the ball and scored again.

The Greenville girls looked terrified. Their tiny point guard brought the ball up the court and hurriedly passed it off to a teammate, who tried to lob it into the paint. Lexi picked off the pass, then turned and fired down the court to an already sprinting Chloe, who laid it in. Less than a minute into the game, 6 to 0, and Greenville called a timeout.

James was all praise, no critique. He encouraged the girls and then sent them back out on the floor, before the timeout was even over.

"Can you not play Victoria?"

"What?"

"Victoria doesn't want to go in. She's freaking out."

James leaned toward her. "You need to talk her into it. I'm putting her in shortly. Convince her."

"Why?"

James looked annoyed. "Because I don't want her associating abuse with basketball. They are two separate things. We need to get her back on the court as soon as possible. Go get her ready."

Emily didn't understand, but James appeared unwilling to negotiate. Emily returned to her seat. "So, you're going in soon."

"What? No!"

"No, really, it's OK. You're going to be great. This isn't about Milton. This is about playing a sport you love, a sport you're good at. This is about you helping your team to bring home another gold ball." Emily couldn't even believe she'd said the words, but they worked.

Victoria gave her a nearly inaudible "OK." Then, when James called her name seconds later, without hesitation, she trotted to the scorer's table to check in.

After the calm, nurturing, and supportive half-time talk, James led the girls back out onto the court. Sydney Hopkins's father was standing behind the bench waiting for them.

"Can I talk to you?" he asked James as they approached.

The school board member made a big show of turning his back on Emily so he could speak to the coach in the middle of a playoff game.

The conversation didn't last long and Mr. Hopkins didn't look satiated as he indignantly returned to his seat.

James sat beside Emily.

"What was that all about?" Emily muttered.

"Don't worry about it."

"It was about me."

He looked at her. "Really. Don't worry about it."

Greenville fell to the mighty Lady Panthers 55 to 23. The girls burst into celebration. The crowd began to noisily spill out of the seats. James loosened his tie.

"Congratulations, Coach," Emily said. "Now what?"

"Now we go get Chinese food. Then we go home and practice. We've got a big game Thursday."

"Against Rangeley?"

"Not yet. We've got to get past the winner of two versus six first."

"Who is two and six?"

"Valley versus Vinalhaven," he said, his eyes sparkling.

James claimed he didn't care about basketball anymore, but his new shoes sure did seem to be a snug fit.

MacKenzie appeared beside them. "Congratulations, Mr. Gagnon."

"Thank you, MacKenzie. How are you doing?"

"Well, this might not be a good time to ask, and I completely understand if the answer is no, in fact, I'll even be OK if the answer is no, so don't worry about devastating me—"

"Yes," James said.

MacKenzie looked at him, confused.

"The answer is yes. We practice Monday at ten."

She jumped up and down like a little kid at Christmas. "Thank you! Thank you!" She looked as if she wanted to hug him, then decided against it, and hurried off toward her mom, who was waiting only twenty feet away.

Emily waved to her, and she smiled, looking relieved. Emily turned to James. "Ten in the morning? Why so early?"

"Our next game will be at ten. Got to get used to playing in the morning."

# Chapter 38

James asked Emily to attend practice. "Bring a book. You don't even have to do anything, unless someone has a meltdown."

"Are you sure you need me?" She wasn't averse to helping; she just really didn't think it necessary.

"The school building will be empty, and I don't think I should be alone with them," he said matter-of-factly, and she thought he might have a point. This was the man who wouldn't cross her threshold.

"I wonder if they should've asked a woman to finish coaching the season," she said. "No offense," she hastily added.

"None taken. And I'm pretty sure they did ask a woman. Or three. I know I wasn't their first choice. I'm just the one who said yes."

"You've said that before. It seems like everyone would want to coach this team. Doesn't everyone love basketball? And they all sure seem to know the rules when they're screaming at the refs. I would think people would've been fighting for the job."

"It was the day before tournaments started. No one wanted to suffer the wrath of the island if they lost."

"But you don't mind island wrath?"

He smiled. "I kind of enjoy it."

She couldn't tell whether he was kidding.

She did bring a book, *The Visitation* by Peretti, and the first practice was entirely uneventful. No meltdowns. No one needed her.

Having finished *The Visitation*, she brought *Stardust* by Gaiman to the second practice, and found her favorite school board member sitting in the bleachers.

When she and James walked in, he stood. "Why is she here?" PeeWee Hopkins spat.

Emily snuck a look at Sydney. She looked a mile beyond embarrassed. Emily smiled at her.

"It's an open practice," James said. "Anyone can be here. You're welcome to stay as well."

Emily found her spot on the bleachers and opened her book. She stared down at the page and tried to ignore the burning sensation in her neck and cheeks.

"She's not even going to have a job by Monday. Doesn't she know that?"

"She does not know that. And neither do you. And I'd be careful what you say about her. She didn't do anything wrong, PeeWee. She reported a crime. She did something that made your daughter safer. You should be thanking her."

"Oh for Pete's sake. I've known Milton his entire life. So have you. He didn't do anything. You should be standing beside him, not beside your stuck-up girlfriend."

James began to walk away. "I've got to get to practice. You have a nice day."

Emily felt the man's eyes on her as he left the gym. A single fat tear landed on the paperback's page, and she wiped at her eye with the back of her hand.

After practice, James invited her out to lunch. She gratefully accepted. She could use some emotional eating. At lunch, though, he asked her if she would go to the Rangeley game with him that night.

She groaned.

"You don't have to."

"No, I will. I mean, I want to, because I want to spend time with you, but I'm just a little sick of basketball."

He smiled. "And you've only been hore for one season. Come with me tonight. I'll owe you one. I'll buy the nachos. You can read a book during the game."

"OK. Sounds like a plan. Why do we even have to go, though?"

"I need to see their offense, and their defense for that matter. We played at Rangeley this year, so I didn't see them play. I can't imagine how they beat us the first time, but I've got to make sure it doesn't happen again."

"Chloe."

"What?"

"Chloe is how they beat us last time. MacKenzie had just quit. Chloe wasn't used to playing point guard. They had an awful press, and Chloe couldn't get the ball past it." She took a sip of her water.

James guffawed. "Look at you, Miss Assistant Coach! How do you know all this?"

She shrugged. "I don't really. I mean, I don't understand it. I'm just telling you what Chloe told me. But we've got MacKenzie back now, right? So she can just dribble through the defense?"

He nodded thoughtfully. "Maybe. I've got to see this press."

The press was impressive. The Rangeley girls seemed to have boundless amounts of fiery energy and they too seemed able to use telepathy. They weren't as smooth or organized as the Piercehaven girls, but they made up for their lack of grace with incredible hustle and bustle. All five girls seemed to be everywhere at once. Jumping. Diving. Waving hands in frustrated faces.

"I can see how it happened," Emily muttered.

"Yep, and I can see how it won't happen again."

"How's that?"

"We can't let them control the pace. They like it manic. I don't see how, but they do. We've got to slow it down. Frustrate them. *Bore* them even."

# Chapter 39

On Thursday morning, half the Civic Center was bathed in Valley blue, the other half in red and white.

The Lady Panthers seemed far less nervous and emotional this time around. They appeared to be simply taking care of business.

"Don't get cocky," James cautioned them. "We've got to beat Valley before we can even look at that gold ball."

"We're not cocky," Chloe said, "but we've got MacKenzie back now." She put her arm around her cousin's shoulders. "We can't lose."

James nodded. "Well let's pretend for a moment that we can, and play accordingly." He put his hand out, signaling them all to do the same.

Their hands flew straight up as they all shouted "Piercehaven!" and then they went to line up behind the papered hoop.

On their way to the bench, James whispered to Emily, "I just got an alert on my phone. Other women have come forward, older victims of Milton's, from years ago."

Emily gasped. "Your phone alerts you to that stuff?"

"I programmed it just for his name, so I'd hear if there was any progress on the case. But I don't want any of the girls to know. So don't let them near any electronics during the game."

"Hoping they'll be too busy," she said.

"Yeah. Me too."


Lexi was having the game of her career. She had fifteen points by halftime. In the locker room, James praised her and then said, "Right now their coach is telling them how to shut you down. They're going to double team you. If they do, don't get frustrated, and don't get selfish. Don't force anything. If two girls are guarding you, someone's open. Look for a guard. Maybe it's time to unleash Chloe's three-point shot.

It was time.

Lexi did exactly as she was told. MacKenzie bounced the ball into the post, the defense collapsed in on Lexi, and she kicked it back out to Chloe, who didn't even hesitate. Nothing but net, and the ref held two arms up.

Two possessions later, it happened again, and Valley's coach called a timeout.

Emily figured he was going to stop double teaming Lexi, but she was wrong. All they did was change who Lexi's second defender would be. Chloe was no longer open. Now MacKenzie was. This was a mistake. MacKenzie scored the next four points of the game.

Valley never stood a chance.

The Lady Panthers had done it again. They were going to the Southern Maine finals. They would face Rangeley again, and this time, they would have their skipper at the helm.

At practice Friday, James put in the new press break. Some of the girls balked. It was *nothing* like Milton's press break, after all, which they'd been running since they were five. But most of them took the update in stride.

"You girls are Piercehaven's only hope, now," James called out as they ran through the play. The boys had lost their semifinal game. "If the island is going to get a gold ball this year, we're going to have to beat

Rangeley. And we can't beat Rangeley without breaking their press."

Once they appeared to have it down pat, James put pinnies on seven of his subs. "You guys are the press," he said.

"All *seven* of them?" Chloe said.

"Yes. Rangeley moves fast enough to be seven girls on the court." He looked at his new defense. "Anyone who deflects the ball gets a point. Anyone who steals the ball gets five points. Anyone who gets to twenty points gets an ice cream sundae after practice. Miss Morse, please keep track of the points."

Surprised, Emily snapped her paperback shut and dug through her purse for paper and pen.

"What do we get?" Chloe whined.

"You get to beat Rangeley tomorrow. Ready? Set it up."

He ran them ragged. The pinnied press seemed to be having the time of their lives. It only took Sydney about five minutes to get her twenty points.

"I had no idea you could play defense like that, Syd," James said.

"You promised me ice cream."

The defense laughed. The offense was breathing too hard to laugh. Eighth grader Zoe Lane was the next to earn ice cream.

"Nice job, Zoe! You are quick!"

She beamed. It occurred to Emily that she'd never seen that child smile before.

# Chapter 40

Rangeley's colors were green and white, so the Civic Center looked like a giant Christmas party, where only nachos and steamed hot dogs were served.

The girls seemed more nervous than they had against Valley, but they were still quite composed. Emily, on the other hand, thought she was going to be sick. And she hadn't even had any of the nachos. She was nervous for James. She was nervous for the girls. She couldn't believe how badly she wanted them to win. Voices in her head were arguing. Voice 1: They *need* this. Voice 2: No they don't. It's just a game. Voice 1: That's not true and you know it. They *need* this.

Jasmine lost the jump, which Emily, judging by the look on Jasmine's face, was certain had never happened before. Just like that, Piercehaven was down by two.

Chloe grabbed the ball and quickly inbounded to MacKenzie, who instantly had three girls on her. They were like spring mosquitoes. MacKenzie tried to pivot, but ran into a girl, which knocked her off balance. She tried to look for a way out, but there were hands in her face. The ref's hand was counting down the seconds, and MacKenzie panicked and called a timeout.

She ran over to the bench. "I'm so sorry, Coach. I didn't know what else to do. I didn't want to turn it over."

James squatted down so he was looking up at her. "Look at me," he said.

She did.

"It doesn't matter. That was a great move on your part. This time, try to get rid of the ball a little quicker. But MacKenzie ..." He waited for her to listen. "Really. Great job. Don't sweat it."

The girls trotted out on the floor. Chloe inbounded the ball to MacKenzie, who instantly bounced it back to Chloe, who fired it toward Hailey at half court. There was only one defender between Hailey and her basket and she began to drive, but then apparently remembered her new coach's strategy and took a step back. She stood at the three-point line, dribbling, as the rest of her team joined her and the defense recovered. Her defender looked at her strangely as if to say, "What are you doing?"

Hailey passed the ball to MacKenzie at the top of the key, who also stood there, dribbling. Bounce, bounce, bounce. Nothing was happening. Nobody moved. Just the ball going up and down beneath MacKenzie's sure hand. Just the head of MacKenzie's defender going up and down, her eyes glued to the ball. She looked a little like an intensely focused bobblehead.

There is no shot clock in high school basketball.

Bounce, bounce, bounce. Finally, MacKenzie's defender couldn't take it anymore; she lunged for the ball, and MacKenzie expertly scooted past her. Jasmine's defender left her to help, and MacKenzie scooped the ball to Jasmine, who laid it in.

And so it began. The slow march to victory.

Piercehaven did not press Rangeley. They played a zone. At practice, Chloe had said that she hadn't played in a zone since junior high. James had said, "And on Saturday night, you will again."

It worked. The Rangeley offense came screaming down the floor and tried to drive into the key, where they hit a red wall. The ball squirted loose and MacKenzie came up with it. She got it across half court quickly, before the mosquitos could settle on her, but then she slowed down. And waited.

Nearly a full minute later, Piercehaven scored again and took the lead. For good.

When the final whistle blew, the scoreboard read 26 to 18—the lowest scoring game of the season. The girls jumped into one giant group hug and then Hailey and Chloe ran to cut down one net, while Lexi and Jasmine ran to the other. Stepladders appeared out of nowhere and the girls climbed them.

Suddenly, Lexi and Jasmine stopped cutting and looked down at their teammates. Jasmine motioned for Victoria to come forward. Victoria did. Jasmine descended the ladder and motioned for Victoria to climb.

Lexi and Victoria cut down the net together, and then took turns waving it in the air. Their smiles were huge. Hundreds of cameras flashed, capturing those smiles forever.

Hailey Leadbetter was named most valuable player of the tournament. She accepted the trophy with tears streaming down her cheeks.

Tears streamed down Emily's cheeks as well. She didn't even know exactly why she was crying. It was just all so beautiful.

# Chapter 41

Emily was in an unusually good mood on her way to work Monday morning. She was usually in a good mood, but this was above and beyond. Even though the sky was gray, even though it was only ten degrees out, even though vacation was over, she still felt as if she were skipping through a field of tulips.

She walked into the building with a spring in her step and a smile on her face. Mr. Hogan met her at the door. "Please come into my office."

Something in his tone made her smile fade, but not entirely disappear, so she was still grinning when she sat down and he shut the door behind her.

He didn't even wait until he sat down. On his way to the chair, he said, "I'm afraid we're going to have to let you go."

The grin faded, but absurdly, most of the joy did not. She thought she must have misunderstood.

"I'm sorry?"

"Please don't make this more difficult than it already is. I warned you against trying to convert your students. You ignored my warnings. So you're done here. Go to your room and—"

"I didn't try to convert anyone!"

"Miss Morse, have some dignity. Multiple people saw you actually *praying* with the basketball team in the Augusta Civic Center."

Emily was fairly certain no one had seen that. She was also certain it didn't matter.

"You were a probationary hire. Your probation period is now over. I am not even obligated to give you a reason for your dismissal, but I am giving you one, as I'm hoping it will help you to make better decisions in your next job. How you respond to this dismissal will affect what we will say when people call for references."

"Is this about Milton?"

Mr. Hogan appeared to be focusing on a spot on the wall just above and behind her head. "This has nothing to do with that situation. I told you, this is about you violating the students' basic right to a separation of church and state."

Emily knew that he was misusing this bit of history, but she figured it would be pointless to point that out.

He looked at the clock. "Please go gather your things. I want you out of here before first bell. Good luck to you, Miss Morse." He turned to his computer. She stood to go.

She made it halfway down the hallway before the tears came. She didn't even have a box or a bag to put her things in. She wondered if she was in shock. The hallway was covered in red and white streamers, but she didn't even notice.

"What's wrong?" Thomas asked as soon as she entered the room.

"Could you go find me a garbage bag or a box?" she asked.

"Did you get fired?"

She looked at him, nodded, and forced a smile. "It's all good. God is in control."

"Is this because of Milton?" Chloe asked. "Did you know he's confessed?"

"I didn't know that, and they say it's not because of Milton."

"What else could it be?" she asked. Tears were swimming in her eyes now too.

"Thomas, I could really use a trash bag."

"No. I'll help you carry stuff to the car. Just make piles."

She did. She made piles. And Chloe and Thomas helped her carry them. Kids in the hallway turned and watched them walk out.

"What's going on?" Hailey asked, but no one answered her.

They met Kyle in the hallway. He went out of his way to avoid eye contact. It was as if they'd never met.

The fresh air, even though it was piercingly cold, was a welcoming refreshment to Emily's lungs. She gulped it down as she headed to her car.

She dropped her books and her bag in the backseat and then turned to hug Thomas. She held him for several seconds. "Thanks for being so awesome, Thomas. You made my time here so much richer." She let go of him and then wrapped her arms around Chloe. "Chloe, my dear, I absolutely adore you. I'll see you at church." She let go and looked at Thomas again. "I'd sure like to see you at church too."

"Yeah, yeah."

She climbed into her car and shut the door, sniffing madly. Between the cold and the crying, her nose had become a faucet.

Thomas rapped on the window.

She started the car and rolled her window down.

"My step-mom is on the school board," he said. "I'm going to fix this."

She didn't know what to say, so she just nodded, and then drove away.

Her landlord's car was parked in her driveway, and she became painfully aware that it probably wasn't her driveway anymore. She took a deep breath and tried to compose herself. She found it wasn't so hard—her sadness was being ousted by anger.

Lauren met her at the door. "I'm sorry, Emily."

This wasn't what Emily had expected to hear, and she looked at her in surprise.

"MacKenzie really liked you. I'm sorry it didn't work out. And I hate to ask you this, but could you be out of here by tonight? Don't worry about cleaning or anything. We'll take care of that."

Emily looked at her, her jaw slack.

"Sorry, don't mean to rush you. We just need to get the house ready. The new teacher will be here tomorrow."

*New teacher? How could they possibly have moved so fast?* Then it hit her. *They've been planning this for a while.* "Lauren, can you tell me, off the record, what the real reason is?"

Lauren sighed. "There isn't one. Or there's a thousand. Sometimes people just don't work out here. The island is strange. If people don't like you, there's not much you can do to change things."

"But people *do* like me. At least, the kids do."

"Well, I'm sorry, someone didn't." Past tense. As if it was already over. A done deal. "I'll leave you to it," she said, and stepped outside without looking back.

# Chapter 42

It took her a few hours to pack. She couldn't believe how much stuff she had accumulated in just six months. When she had crammed all her belongings into the trunk and backseat, and set Daisy and Nick in front, she left the keys on the kitchen table and walked out. She resisted the urge to look around and say her goodbyes. She didn't trust herself not to have a complete meltdown.

She drove to James's house and knocked on the door. He answered in a ratty T-shirt and pajama pants. His hair was tousled and he needed a shave. His appearance cheered her up immensely.

"What's wrong?"

"I've just been fired," she said, her voice cracking on that last syllable.

"Oh, you're kidding. Come in," he said, and stepped back.

"Seriously?" She raised an eyebrow.

"Yes, seriously. Get in here. Let me take your coat."

She gave it to him and then glanced around the small home, which was neat as a pin.

"Have a seat."

She sat on the couch.

"What happened?"

"I don't even know. Mr. Hogan said it was because I prayed with the girls in Augusta—"

"What?"

"But I know that's not it. Maybe it's all the Milton stuff, though Chloe said he's confessed?"

"He did. Saw it on my phone."

"How do you have cell service when no one else does?"

"I don't. I have WiFi." He tried to smooth out the legs of his pajama pants as if he was wearing slacks and then leaned back in his chair. "They offered him some kind of deal. It's not official yet, but apparently he's going to do about ten years."

"Ten years?" She couldn't believe it, but she actually felt sympathy for Milton.

"Yeah, well, you can't have sex with fourteen-year-olds you're supposed to be educating. Now, back to you, what do you want to do?"

"There's not much I can do—"

"There's the union?"

"Yeah, but what are they going to do? I don't even have a real contract."

He nodded thoughtfully. "Do you want to fight it?"

"Kind of, but I don't want to waste my time and energy either. I don't think I can win. I don't even really know what or whom I'm fighting."

"Well, you're fighting PeeWee Hopkins, school board member, Milton's second cousin. And you're fighting the more than a hundred other Milton relatives on this island."

"So you don't think it's about the praying?"

"I don't think it's about the praying. I don't think the girls would have said anything, and no one else was there. Besides, you didn't tell them they had to pray." He paused, and then nudged her foot with his. "Hey, you're still the assistant basketball coach. I know it doesn't pay much, but …"

She started crying again, and she didn't even know why. "I don't know, James. I don't know if I can go back in that gym."

"You mean the cafeteria?"

She laughed through her tears. Then she leveled a gaze at him. "I don't want to leave the island, James. I don't want to leave you."

He took a deep breath, looked around the room, and then returned her gaze. "I didn't really want to have this conversation in my pajamas, Em, but here goes. I don't want you to leave the island either. In fact, I'm asking you not to. I don't have a ring and I'm not going to propose in my pajamas, but you ride this out, and I will propose marriage properly. I make enough money fishing to support us. You won't have to teach. You could still work with the kids through the church.

This struck her as both good and bad news. James wanted to marry her: the best news ever. She didn't need to teach: not so great news. She *wanted* to teach. She had *always* wanted to teach.

James apparently couldn't read her reaction. "Or if you don't want a proposal, we can do that too."

She gasped. "No, of course I want to marry you, James. I'm madly in love with you. I'm just surprised is all. I wasn't expecting you to say all that."

James leaned forward and reached a hand out toward Emily. She reached out and took it. They sat like that for several seconds, four feet apart, holding hands, gazing into each other's eyes. "I owe you an apology," he said, letting go of her hand. "I was hesitant to let myself fall for you. I mean, I was crazy about you from day one, but I tried not to be."

She frowned.

"What I mean is, I didn't think you'd last. Teachers don't last here. I figured you'd be gone by Christmas—"

"You were almost right."

"Well, I figured you'd leave of your own accord. And I didn't want to have to choose between you and the island. I didn't want to have to make that choice. I didn't think I *could* make that choice." He looked at the wall for several seconds.

She resisted the urge to say something just to fill the pause.

Still looking at the wall, he said, "I cared about another woman once. Her name was Naomi. She came for a summer. I fell for her. And when summer was over, she left. She left like it wasn't any big deal, like she expected me to come with her. I didn't even have my own boat yet, but I still couldn't do it. I didn't *want* to do it. I mean, I *really* cared about her, but I just couldn't leave."

He finally looked at her again. "I know that's weird. But that's how you found me. Alone at thirty-two, living on an almost-deserted island." He forced a chuckle.

"It's not weird."

He looked grateful. "Emily, I'd like to think that if you had to leave this island that I could go with you. I would even try. I just don't know if I could. My traps are here. My boat is here. My *life* is here. I don't know how to exist anywhere else."

"James, I'm not going to ask you to leave. I love it here. I'd love it a lot more if I still had a job, but still, I love you, and I will stay here."

James looked at her thoughtfully. Then he softly said, "I love you too. And I'm sorry it took me so long to say it." He slapped his knees. "But right now, let's get you home. We've been in here alone too long." He stood.

"Uh, James? I can't go home."

"Why?"

"They kicked me out."

"Already?"

She shrugged, trying to look cool and nonchalant. "The perils of free rent?"

He looked around thoughtfully. "Well, you can't stay here."

*Obviously*.

"Let's go see Abe," he said.

"Seriously?"

"Yeah, they've got a guest room."

# Chapter 43

Abe and Lily welcomed a distraught Emily and her two cats into their home and upstairs into their comfortable guest room. Left alone, she tried to read the Bible, tried to pray, but ended up watching television instead. Thinking just seemed too exhausting.

After four episodes of *Jericho*, James asked her to go to basketball practice. She felt guilty saying no, but she declined his offer.

Lily invited her downstairs for dinner. It was delicious, the company was loving, and no one talked about the big, fat, recently-terminated elephant in the room.

After dinner, she went back to *Jericho*, until she fell asleep.

What felt like only minutes later, she was awoken by a knock on her door. She looked around, disoriented. Morning sunlight spilled through the thin, white curtains. The TV was still on, showing an "Are you still watching *Jericho*?" message.

"Come in!" she croaked.

Lily opened the door and peeked in, looking distraught.

"What's wrong?" Emily asked.

"I don't think anything's wrong. But James is downstairs. He says he needs you right away. He says to dress nicely."

"Dress nicely?" she repeated, annoyed. "For what?"

"I don't know, but he says to hurry." She shut the door, and Emily heard her feet go down the carpeted stairs.

Emily dragged herself out of bed and went about the business of making herself presentable. She skipped the makeup and jewelry
though, as she couldn't imagine needing such frills at 8:15 in the morning. She grabbed her coat and followed Lily's path down the stairs.

James was waiting just inside the door. He was positively beaming. Emily couldn't imagine why he was so happy. Then she realized, *He must have gotten the ring. Maybe I should've put on makeup.*

"Come on," he said, reaching for her hand, "we've got to hurry."

She let him take her hand and pull her out into the cold, and what a cold morning it was. She gasped. "What's the temperature?"

"The bank thermometer said zero, but it's got to be at least twenty below with wind chill."

She shuddered in her coat and hurried toward the running pickup. When they had both climbed in, she asked, "James, what's going on? I need coffee."

"No time."

*What on earth?*

He drove toward the school.

"James, where are we going?"

He didn't answer, just kept smiling foolishly.

They were almost to the school when she noticed a news van. "Oh no, more Milton drama?"

"I don't think so," James said enigmatically.

Emily rolled her eyes. Then they came up over the knoll and she saw something crazy. Something so crazy, she didn't understand what she was looking at.

It appeared that every student in the high school was standing in front of the front doors, and they were holding hands. "James," she said breathlessly, "what is this?"

He pulled into a parking spot and shut off the engine. "Come on."

She climbed out of the truck and let him take her hand again. He led her toward the students, who spontaneously burst into applause at the sight of her. She smiled at

284

them; even though she had no idea what they were doing, or why they were cheering, she smiled. It was just a habit, smiling at her students.

Suddenly there was a microphone and camera in her face. "What do you think of this display of support, Miss Morse?" the reporter asked.

Emily blinked in surprise. "How did you know to get here for this?" she asked. It was a bit nonsensical, but the budding islander within her wondered how a news van knew to catch the first ferry.

"The girls basketball team planned this last night," the reporter answered.

Emily looked at James. "Did you do this?"

He put his free hand up in the air in protest. "No, ma'am. I had no idea this was happening until just a few minutes ago, when Chloe called me. She was going to go get you herself, but there was no one at your house."

Emily looked around wide-eyed.

"So how does this make you feel?" the reporter prodded.

"I don't really know," Emily stammered. "I don't think I understand what's happening."

"Miss Morse," the reporter said in an overly dramatic voice, "the female basketball players have organized a protest in your honor. The high school students are refusing to go to class—"

"Oh no," Emily interrupted. "They need to go to class. Plus it's freezing out here!"

The reporter continued, "And the girls basketball team is refusing to play in the state game until you are reinstated."

"What?" Emily cried. She had never been so shocked in her whole life. The tears began to fall as the meaning of the scene before her sank in.

"Can you tell us why you were let go, Miss Morse?"

Emily shook her head, not because she didn't want to tell them, but because she didn't really know.

"We're getting conflicting reports, Miss Morse. Some say it was because you tried to share your Christian beliefs with students, but some say it's because of the role you played in Milton Darling's arrest?"

Emily looked at her. "I really don't know why I was let go. But can we get these students inside? It's really cold out here."

"Administration has already tried, but you can certainly speak to them." The reporter made a sweeping gesture toward the small mob of shivering students.

Emily walked toward them, gave them another of her teacher smiles, and then loudly spoke, "I can't even tell you all how touched I am by this show of support. I love each and every one of you, and I think you know that. But right now I need something else from you. The best thing you can do for me is to go inside, get warm, and go to class. You have made your statement, and I'm grateful. Now go find a register and sit by it!"

Emily was amazed and delighted to see the students looking at Thomas, as if for some kind of leadership. But Thomas was staring thoughtfully at Emily. He gave her a small smile; then he nodded, and students began filing toward the door.

Hailey walked toward Emily, and her teammates followed. "We're not playing the game, Miss Morse. Not unless they give you a contract, right here and now, for this year and next year. We've already told the principal and the school board members. You can't change our minds."

Emily found it difficult to breathe. "We'll talk about that later. Please, go get warm."

Hailey gave her a hug, and then led her teammates inside.

Emily looked at James. "Well, I've got to say, I didn't see that coming."

The microphone was back in her face. "What are your thoughts, Miss Morse?"

Emily wiped away her tears. "My thoughts? I think that these students are amazing. And I think that schools have a hard time knowing which new teachers to keep. I think this school, this time, has made a mistake in not keeping me, but I don't hold that against them. They were just trying to do what is best for their students." She smiled and tried to walk away, but was approached by an attractive, impeccably-groomed woman she didn't recognize.

"Hi," she said, stepping between Emily and the reporter. "I'm Abby, Thomas's stepmom. Would you please step inside?" Emily nodded and headed toward the door. Abby looked at James. "You can come too, James."

A blessed gust of warm air hit them as soon as they stepped inside. Abby led them to the conference room, where Emily had wrestled with Milton so long ago. Today, the large table was surrounded by school board members, including landlords Lauren and Mike, as well as Sydney's father, PeeWee.

"Please come in, Miss Morse," Mr. Hogan said. "Have a seat."

There was only one chair. Emily sat in it. James leaned against the wall behind her.

She had no idea what was about to happen, but she felt safer knowing James was there.

"We have a proposal for you, Miss Morse, but we want to make it crystal clear that this proposal has nothing to do with the student spectacle you just witnessed outside. Those students just embarrassed our school and will be disciplined accordingly."

Abby shot Mr. Hogan a glare, and he looked sheepish as he continued, "My concern here is the academic welfare of these students, and it has come to my attention that our language arts MAPE scores have drastically improved since you began teaching here. So, we'd like to offer you a contract, for this year, and next."

Abby slid a contract across the table to Emily.

# Chapter 44

The official program for the Class D State Championship game listed Emily Morse as assistant coach. This struck her as unreasonably funny.

The girls were downright relaxed, maybe even a bit silly, as they ran through their warm-up routine. "Next year, I'm choosing the warm-up music," James grumbled from the seat beside her.

She looked at him in surprise. "Are you coaching next year?"

"They've asked me to. Want to be my assistant?"

"Not really."

He laughed. "Well, think it over."

The Lady Panthers were playing the undefeated Northern Maine champs, Katahdin High School. They were a well-coached team with two girls over six feet tall. It wouldn't be a cakewalk.

But no one had told Hailey that. She scored six points before Katahdin double-teamed her, but even that didn't slow her down. Somehow, she managed to spin out of each trap and head right for the paint, where she either scooped the ball in, got fouled trying, or scooped the ball in *and* got fouled.

By the end of the half, she had 19 points, 9 of which were from three-point plays.

On the way into the locker room, Chloe said, "I'd call you a ball hog, but I'm enjoying my vacation."

Hailey laughed. "They'll adjust. The second half will be different."

Except that it wasn't. Katahdin tried to shut Hailey down, but they just couldn't. On the rare occasion that she did miss, Katahdin got the rebound every single time, but Hailey didn't miss much.

Katahdin went ahead halfway through the third quarter thanks to two quick three-pointers, but then James put Sydney in for Chloe. On her way by, he grabbed her shoulder and said, "You drive that shooter *crazy*, you understand? I want you all over her!"

Sydney did as instructed, and the hot shooter never got another shot off.

# PIERCEHAVEN

Just before the end of the third quarter, Hailey cut through the paint, MacKenzie led her with the pass, and Hailey hit a fade-away jumper to take the lead back.

The Lady Panthers never looked back.


Again they jumped and laughed and danced around the floor, with the basketball nets around their necks. They calmed down and appeared humble as they received the gold ball and then they held it up in the air and started screaming with unabashed joy.

As Hailey made her way to the locker room, reporters stopped her. "You played a great game today, Hailey. What were you thinking about during the game?"

Hailey's smile was confident and dazzling. "I was just thinking, 'Man, this is *fun*!'"

The reporter laughed. "So you were feeling pretty confident then? No nerves?"

Hailey's eyes grew serious, but her smile stayed. "Oh, there's always nerves. You know, as a team, we've been through a lot this year, but we've had great coaches, Coach Gagnon and Miss Morse, and they just really helped to keep us calm and confident. It's hard not to be victorious when you've got people like them behind you."

# Large Print Books by Robin Merrill

## Piercehaven Trilogy
Piercehaven
Windmills
Trespass

## New Beginnings
Knocking
Kicking
Searching

## Shelter Trilogy
Shelter
Daniel
Revival

## Wing and a Prayer Mysteries
The Whistle Blower
The Showstopper
The Pinch Runner
The Prima Donna

**Gertrude, Gumshoe Cozy Mystery Series**
Introducing Gertrude, Gumshoe
Gertrude, Gumshoe: Murder at Goodwill
Gertrude, Gumshoe and the VardSale Villain
Gertrude, Gumshoe: Slam Is Murder
Gertrude, Gumshoe: Gunslinger City
Gertrude, Gumshoe and the Clearwater Curse

Want the inside scoop?
Visit robinmerrill.com to join
Robin's Readers!

*Robin also writes sweet romance
as Penelope Spark:*

**Sweet Country Music Romance**
The Rising Star's Fake Girlfriend
The Diva's Bodyguard
The Songwriter's Rival

**Clean Billionaire Romance**
The Billionaire's Cure
The Billionaire's Secret Shoes
The Billionaire's Blizzard
The Billionaire's Chauffeuress
The Billionaire's Christmas

Made in the USA
Las Vegas, NV
08 December 2020